Having studied professional make-up art, interior and graphic design, Jennifer went on to sculpt Disney toys, Wedgewood collectables and mad things for cereal boxes, she also worked in the creature departments on *Harry Potter and the Philosopher's stone*, and *The Mummy Returns*.

When not writing, Jennifer is a sculptor currently living on the Isle of Wight in the UK.

ALYONS

Volume 2

SPARKS ON THE KNIFE EDGE

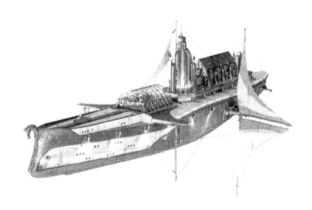

JENNIFER MARTIN

ISBN: 97987 19914176

SDG

THE STORY SO FAR...

The star ship, Copernicus, has crossed 642 light years of space, from the planet Aleyo. By surfing the gravity whirls and waves out in the black, it took her just two months, and now she secretly orbits Earth. Her crew is here to collect plant and animal DNA, so that Alyon farmers, scientists, engineers, and adventurers can build a new and improved world, far from their dying planet. Being extremely curious beings, they have taken to investigating how things here work, however humans have advanced alarmingly, and the quest is waltzing on a knife edge. Fortunately, Alyons are tenacious, and adaptable, and they love an exciting dance... and tea, they do love a spot of tea, and cheese, and going extremely *fast* - but not all at the same time, because though it may be thrilling, it could also be fantastically messy and probably hazardous.

CHAPTER 1

THE FAR SIDE

"We're here," said Zaphine. She flicked the switches to fire the boosters beneath the dropship, to level and slow it. Onboard computers could fly and land the dropship well enough, but Zaphine enjoyed the challenge and simple joy of flying manually. She loved the feeling of being one with the ship; it made her feel like *she* was flying. Truth be told, Zaphine was a better pilot than the computer.

"Watch and learn and don't get crumbs down the seats," she whispered.

Nox nodded and watched and learned. He ate his hot Roddenberry pie carefully to avoid crumbing the seats, and washed it down with an ice cool flask of *pon'dâlgie* - an organic veggie juice.

Gravy dripped down his chin, and a green moustache set across his top lip.

"It's creepy down there," he mumbled, and pointed with a piece of pie crust.

"Creepy or no, we have to check it out, it's why we've come."

A simple remote-controlled probe could have done the job, but live eyes are better at spotting some things, and Captain Zizsou knew that computers don't always deal well with surprises. He also knew that his team was the best of the best. The dropship touched down upon the powdered grey rock. Tiny shards of spiky dust bounced up around the landing supports, and lingered for a moment, before drifting down to the moon surface again. Some dust, drawn by static build up, clung to the ship. There was no wind. There was no air. Nothing moved. The place was as silent as a school hall at midnight, and almost as spooky.

Zaphine pointed at Nox's face, making small circles in the air with her finger.

"You've got green on you."

Nox licked his lips and wiped his face with his sleeve.

"*Aaawnaaw-Nox-not-the-sleeve*, now it'll go everywhere. *Din't* your mum teach you?"

"She did!" Nox laughed and flashed a cheeky green-toothed grin at her, then carefully lowered his diamond-glass fishbowl helmet over his head.

"Ha! You're terrible," Zaphine chuckled and shook her head.

She and Nox pulled on their silver space-onesies, meticulously double-checking and sealing all the joints in the suits, any carelessness at this stage could result in a nasty surprise later.

"It's going to smell funny you know and I don't mean funny-tee-hee."

She braided her hair, then slipped on her helmet. If she didn't tie back her soft, wilful hair, it could spread out and completely fill the helmet. Her head would look like a pink and orange ping pong ball; she'd be unable to see anything except of course, pink and orange hair, which simply wouldn't do.

"I like the smell," muttered Nox.

Nox was not actually keen on smelling weird, few people are, it is just that he was more embarrassed to be caught being ill mannered again. At least it wasn't as bad as being spotted nibbling nose gems and having Hydroponix point and yell, *"YOU PICKED A WINNER!"* Now *that* was mortifying.

They stepped boldly from the Paladin ramp onto the moon surface. He could hear Zaphine humming as she began to take readings and rock samples from the area. His helmet took on a golden hue as it adjusted to the harsh light of the sun, and as his eyes grew accustomed, the sky appeared as black as coal tar. Not a single star was visible. It gave him the *weirdiecreeps*. Nox was irritated and edgy. This lunar expedition felt like a *wild horse floose* - a spectacular waste of time and energy. Prowling around an airless grey desert isn't fun and Nox's formidable imagination began to shape the rocks and fill the shadows. His mind's eye conjured stealthy bogbeasts, *spiceworms*, and all manner of googlies - lurking and creeping.

"No other living things here at all, Nox, you *papoon*, just you and me," laughed Zaphine, "stop freaking yourself out."

His zooty space suit, gold hefty-boots and fishbowl helmet made Nox feel like a complete *noof*. At least Zaphine looked equally ridiculous; this made him feel a little better. A menacing itch began to circle the inside of his left nostril. He flared his nose a few times and sniffed to make it go away. The last time Nox sneezed in his helmet, he spent the

10

day observing wonders of the universe through speckles of spit and a tentacle of snot. *Teagulls* he called them. They weren't as pretty as he made them sound. This was the tenth stop on the far side of the moon, and everything looked the same, the same, *aaand* the same, except for one thing...

"*What is that?*" he pointed.

Perched on a cliff ledge near the top of a craggy mountain, nestled a collection of buildings. The structure was roughly the size of a large bouncy castle, and looked like a fantastical fortress pinned together by Vivienne Westwood in her heyday.

"Great *Gumberguts*! I think it's the ancient Solvaynian spaceport," whispered Zaphine, "I can't believe it is still here, it was supposed to have shut down a millennium ago... a thousand years out of use and it still looks fantastic!" Zaphine held up her BLAC-Adder and scanned it. "Let'sa have a little explore!" And before Nox could say, "Let'sa Not," she galloped slowly back to the ship with great leaping steps.

Nox lingered, watching the structure warily for a moment, then he turned and galloped after her.

"Wait! It could be dangerous!"

As quickly as possible, they reversed the static from their silver suits, to throw off the spikey moon dust, before entering the ship, and within minutes, they were up and circling the citadel.

"Look at it!" whispered Nox. "Are those diamonds?!"

"Can't be. No. Maybe," said Zaphine " I think so. Yes, they are."

"So many," murmured Nox, "high grade by the look."

The surface of the structure glistened with

golden power cables draped across platinum-graphine shield plates, which were encrusted with scarlet, indigo, sea green and white diamonds. Each one a flawless gem, up to five centimetres in width, precision-cut, and carefully placed to direct light down into receptors for harvesting star energy, instead of up and out for showing off. Even so, the whole thing sparkled like a dew-covered spider web catching the early morning sun. Zaphine landed the ship on a high platform and checked the walkway extending to the main building.

"Wild karkinoses couldn't keep me from getting in there," she purred.

"It looks locked."

"Let's go," she whispered.

Nox hesitated, "there could be traps."

"I'm going in."

Zaphine trotted down the Paladin ramp and

skipped lightly onto the long-deserted platform. Nox followed reluctantly. They found an entrance door. It was unlocked. She opened it and they stepped into the airlock chamber, then she closed the door behind them. Scanners analyzed their presence then the chamber sealed and began to fill with air. Scan checks cleared them as mostly harmless and on a console in the corner a row of small red lights began to flash. One by one they turned green and the door leading into the main complex opened. The facility lit up and Zaphine and Nox slinked in. Zaphine scanned the area and checked the air quality then removed her helmet. It was a relief to be out in fresh air.

"This air is fresh!" said Nox, "is it normal for the air smell so fresh after being sealed in for so long? How is there even still air in here?"

Zaphine ignored him.

"Readings show that apart from plants and feral creatures in that garden biome over there, we are definitely alone." She pointed to a group of observation towers, "three working telescopes in those, and some weird constructions in that tower up there. I can't see what they are exactly but there is a *verylot* of power directed there."

Nox felt bolder and began to wander slowly from the entrance area into the main hall of the complex.

The Solvaynians were larger than Alyons, so everything in the complex was as big for the two explorers as adult furniture would be for a toddler. To the human eye, it would make a fantastic Space Barbie or Action man Base. (Your average Alyon would only measure just passed Space Barbie's knee.) The building glowed with pleasant light, and ancient exotic plants grew neatly throughout, creating what could pass as the perfect lair for a computer geek, nature freak, astronomer hermit mastermind.

"It's bizarrely dramatic and sort of peaceful

at the same time, weird how they got that to work..." marveled Zaphine, "and clean, weirdly clean."

"I guess the janitor-bots maintain the place, clearing dust, printing the required atoms to repair damage, that sort of thing. Hey - that's a good name for a *trash* band, *A-tom-ic Damaaaage!*"

Nox whacked at his imaginary air drums for a moment then remembered where he was. He sniffed and holstered his pretend drumsticks in make-believe holsters, then listened for any mysterious noises. There were none. It was so still; Nox could hear both his hearts beating.

"Of course! Repair mechs! Zaphine waved her tablet at the room, "that would explain who has been trimming and recycling the biome plants, and clearing the dust off the diamonds, but... who repairs the repair mechs I wonder?"

"Maybe they repair each other...?"

"Maybe..." said Zaphine.

Nox wandered through the main hall and stopped to gaze out of the enormous viewing portals, at the crisp grey moonscape. The horison looked cut out and pasted on to black sky. He imagined what this place must have been like in the glory days. Ships, scientists and astronauts everywhere, traders and travellers passing through, the hubbub of languages from all over the galaxy and exotic ancient music and the *food!* It made Nox wish time travel were possible.

Zaphine joined him by the window but kept reading her notes.

"While you're at it, Zaph, would you please pick up a selection of historical documents from the computers, so I can build a copy of this place as it was, for the VR goggles?"

"Sure-*ting*. Listen to this, records say the Solvaynian astronomers abandoned the base just over 995 years ago."

"You're telling me no one has been here for 995 years?!" exclaimed Nox. "It looks as if they left yesterday!"

"According to this..." Zaphine flicked over pages of historical documents, "the War of the Exalted Shallot was heating up around that time, I guess there were more urgent matters cooking back on Solvay, and they left in a rush, with the hope of returning one day. They never did."

"Oh," said Nox.

As the pair explored, they passed through blue marble halls laden with decorative tessellations and elegant lighting, and glass rooms crammed with ancient technologies. They imagined the lively atmosphere when the people occupied it, and whilst on their little tour they triggered a proximity sensor. A silent alert went out. The pulse was short-range; it didn't leave the Solar System.

Zaphine was puzzled. "It *is* odd how the

spaceport is still in such good shape. It doesn't feel abandoned, it *feels* like someone is taking care of it.

"*Nah*," said Nox. "*I reckon* they send a janitor once a quinquennium, to tidy and keep it geared up. Ready for operation."

After exploring a little more, Nox and Zaphine added a few canisters of oxygen to the air supply, and gave some of the repair mechs a quick check over and service, then quietly left the place as they found it. Apart from having a priceless space base upon it, the far side of the moon looked very much the same as the near side of the moon. Zaphine and Nox took one last look then took off in their ship, leaving the sparkling citadel behind, and got back to the business of investigating the moon.

The spaceport had indeed been deserted many centuries ago, but as with any useful and beautiful space - someone else quietly moved in. Though the new tenant had not been there for quite some time, they were quite protective of their lair. Visitors were not welcome.

After many hours of measuring and looking at grey rocks, Nox's nerves began to fray. Boredom reared its drab little head and glowered at him; but not for long, because Nox was a master boredom blaster. Nox never stayed bored. He could find fun anywhere, even under the dullest of circumstances. He decided to play in the low gravity. Starting with a slow-gangly run, he launched into three flick-flacks and a wobbly triple Sagan flip, before landing as lightly as a feather, on his feet. He flung out his arms and waved, blowing glorious kisses to his crowds of adoring *imagi*-fans. Zaphine cheered and silently clapped her hands. The dust settled and Nox began to look around for something new to keep his imagination in a happy place. He didn't want to be here exploring the moon. He wanted to be on Earth exploring Italy.

"Ok, Nox. Why Italy?"

"It's electrifying Zaph! When Captain Zizsou describes his days there - the colours, the sounds, the smells, the light, the hustling and bustling, it calls to my soul. I must see it or die a poorer *yon!* I'd give my left ear to hear the music, touch the cloth, smell the perfume, and taste the food. I want to press my hands against the stone... I want to absorb it all."

"You're *bazoinked in the brain*, Nox! More than 500 years have passed since he visited Italy, there are billions of people down there now and they *are* cunning in their weird *humie* way. If one of them nets you, all you'll get is cages and pointy sticks. You'll not like the colours, sounds and smells then, and as for touching cloth, well let's just not go there." She rolled her eyes. "To top it all, I'd have to rescue you and steal back all evidence and dodge humies and fight battle-bots with *frikkin'* laser beams

21

on their *frikkin'* heads, and when my Gra'mar hears of it she will heave a cadenza fit!"

"Let's move on," huffed Nox, causing his fishbowl to momentarily mist up. He bounded up onto a high rock for a better view.

"Here's a good spot. Hold the pimple pie! This is new... Zaph, somebody has been here! Look at these massive boot prints. He jumped into one of the prints and stepped across it. "They're over five times as long as me!"

"Great Groovytash! What made *them?*" Zaphine scanned the area to be certain they were still alone.

Mankind?" suggested Nox.

Zaphine snorted; "now that would be a giant leap, hahaha."

Nox laughed, and then sneezed, and sighed, "oh, *teagulls*."

CHAPTER 2

CAN'T STOP THE SIGNAL

Captain Zizsou paused by the main bridge window, and while he watched the Earth, he sifted through his options. He knew that the moon might still hold a few interesting secrets, but for now it was safer than Earth, and that is what he was more concerned about. Enemy Grumyums being so active in the area was troubling. Grumyums had followed the Copernicus to the Solar System and they were extraordinarily dangerous. He wanted an early warning system set in place before sending his crew back down to the Earth's surface. The continents of the world swept by as the Copernicus orbited and a new day dawned for the second time in an hour. The lift tinged, and Zaphine and Nox stepped smartly on to the bridge to report their safe return from their Moon expedition.

"How was the grand tour?" asked Zizsou. "Did you two find anything interesting?"

"We did," said Nox, casually tossing a perfect red diamond the size of his fist, "we found the abandoned Solvay base, which Zaphine reckons isn't abandoned at all. "

"Someone else has been using that place, I can feel it," whispered Zaphine. "There wasn't anyone anywhere on the moon, but we found pieces of some sort of primitive shuttlecraft out on the big tranquil, flat bit... and a flag. Sparks and stripes on it, blue, white and red. No-one was there, so we took it."

"A flag did you say? That is odd. And ship parts?"

Zizsou knew that had Grumyums been there they would have stripped and smashed everything, so it wasn't them.

"And enormous boot prints," added Nox,

"nothing much else, I'm happy to report that there were no wild googlies about and we got rock samples, and mined a few rubies. No challenge."

"Thank you, Nox. Now, go and get refreshed. You did a great job but you smell funny; incidentally, where is the flag now?"

"Hydro has it." Nox grinned. "He likes it so much..."

Zaphine interrupted with a cackle, "he likes it so much he's making a suit out of it." She flopped back into her pilot seat to check the ship info.

"Captain Zizsou examined the floating 3D map that Nox and Zaphine made of the moon, and mulled over their discoveries. He spoke his thoughts aloud to process them.

"After leaving the abandoned spaceport, you and Nox land over here, at Moon zone 69-7-20," he tapped his finger on the spot, "...and here you find a giant flag with stripes and sparks on it. Who

25

would put a flag with stripes and sparks on the moon? Even if humans could do it, which I doubt, why would they stop there?"

"Tis lunacy!" trilled Zaphine.

"Take us into geosynchronous orbit please Zaph," said Zizsou, "and then, how about a lovely spot of cha?"

"Oooh lovely," said Zaphine, "jasmine green for me please."

The botanical gardens on the Arbor Deck of the Copernicus were cool and lush. A gently cycled breeze brushed the treetops, and all manner of creatures wandered about, grazing and enjoying the moment.

Nox had a quick break, just long enough to eat a toasted cheese and tomato jaffle, then using an AGT - Anti-Gravity Tray, he began the business of moving the moon rocks to Hydroponix's Arbor Lab.

A slinky silver shadow whispered through the treetops, moving swiftly toward him, and then hovered amongst the leaves above.

The moon rocks were heavy, made mostly of silicon, oxygen and iron with traces of other elements thrown in. Nox lifted an armful from the AGT, and placed them carefully onto Hydroponix's rock desk. These rocks had shards of pure ruby running through them; extremely useful for laser tech. Nox would have preferred the Quizats Saddōrax Powerbot to do the heavy lifting, especially when his arm muscles began to gripe, but Hydroponix was doing tests on it.

"*Geeeeves!*" howled Wú, and dropped onto Nox's head, almost flooring him. Eventually, after shifting about like an indecisive transformer wig, he made himself comfortable. Wú, Nox's silver wyvern, adored Nox. The wyvern is a social creature that looks an awful lot like a tiny Birman cat mixed with a Tian Long luck dragon and when Nox came anywhere near to this one, it would stalk him with the single-minded goal of becoming his living snood for as long as possible. Nox laughed and snuggled him. He smelled like puppies, and he was *so fluffy!* Wú showed little interest in the other crew members except for Hydroponix. They were simply over active scenery but Hydroponix was different, he was worth following for the snacks. The robot held zero interest for Wú. Although it walked and talked, he completely ignored it because he knew it wasn't alive. To him it was just a moving machine, like a maintenance mech or walking leaf grinder.

The Copernicus circled the Earth, away from the sun, and now through the roof of the Arbor Deck, the moon was clearly visible. The light reflected from it created a rather dazzling golden twilight. Still sporting his *zazzy* Wú snood, Nox strolled through the garden to Hydroponix's computer desk at the open-air lab. There he found the robot standing with colourful wires sprouting

28

from the shoulders and chest. Hydroponix had attached the cables and was dashing between machines, and tapping excitedly on his BLAC-Adder tablet. The tablet beamed a floating hologram into the air above his desk, showing binary code of green, glowing zeros and ones, running down like tears in the rain.

"Hello Nox. Wot-ho Wú," he declared grandly and took a moment to tickle Wú gently under the chin.

"Geevz!" chirped Wú.

"Nox listen to this it started coming from the robot after I reset the sensors after your moon quest after our return to Earth orbit," babbled Hydroponix.

Nox, tried desperately to concentrate. Wú had squirmed down and was now gleefully circling his neck and purring loudly. He shifted Wú so that he could see what was going on.

"What is it?"

"Nox, truthfully, I don't know. I haven't had breakfast yet. Half my brain can't be trusted and goes back to sleep when I haven't had breakfast. Look here. Our computers work with the range of six harmonic light keys based on the major scale, as you know, whereas this is a binary code using combinations of only these two options - 1 and 0. They work like an on-off switch." He paused and looked up to the heavens, "I'm thinking Maryberry jam, on a hot skön with *thicked* cream and red-leaf cha on the side." Hydroponix looked at the robot and pressed "INPUT" on his device.

"Nothing," he mumbled, "dial the amplifier up one beyond ten please Nox, if you would be so kind? I can't pin this thing down."

"How is that? Any good?"

"No, not a bit," said Hydroponix. He was flummoxed. "It's not echo so let's try this. If I reroute the logic circuit via that cable there... *aaand....* No change."

"Here, try this," said Nox, handing him a honeyseed bar, carefully keeping it beyond licking range of Wú's artful tongue. Then Nox turned over a bucket, sat on it, and listened.

"Thanks," said Hydroponix, unwrapping the colourful waxed cloth that held the snack. He used a precision quarter-inch plotinker to slowly scratch an itch on his ankle inside his boot while he bit into the honeyseed bar and watched the robot. Taking careful aim with the plotinker, he swung it through the air and whacked the robot hard on the head with a loud '*Ka -PAnnngg!*' He waited. No response. He stared at his tablet. "These signals are sophisticated but there are no other galactic vessels within two million kilometres, and they are not coming from this ship. Nox, this makes no sense!" Hydroponix pressed more buttons, and stopped. The evidence was there all along, so obvious. He dropped the honeyseed bar.

"Hah! There are no other galactic vessels around here... except that one!" he spun and pointed the plotinker at the Earth. "These signals are coming from there!"

Wú floated down and made soft chuckling noises as he began to munch on the discarded seed bar. Nox stared at the Earth.

"Can you vector in on the source?"

"Nerp," said Hydroponix, scratching his stomach and frowning, "it's across the planet! They really shouldn't be this advanced yet... but here they are."

"Across the whole planet!"

"Yerp," chuckled Hydroponix, with an excited little head jiggle, using his bino-goggles he gazed up through the crystal ceiling, at Earth.

"Sparky Mullets, Nox, the humans have a global communications network!"

"Can you decode it?" asked Nox.

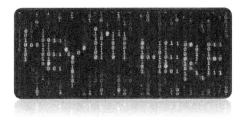

"No, little chap-fella. Until we know how the system operates, I can't make bums or crowns of it. However, if we get down there and actually connect to the network on Earth, we should be able to figure out how it works. This is impressive!"

"I'm taller than you," said Nox.

"Eh?"

"I'm taller than you, you're the little chap-fella."

"Not taller than my hair." declared

Hydroponix defiantly. He sniffed the air - 'SNIFF-SNIFF' - "Can you smell that, Nox?"

Wú looked up and sniffed.

"It wasn't me," protested Nox.

Hydroponix grinned, "I think, I smell a mission!"

"You're a devious little chap-fella, Mr. Kai," laughed Nox. "You're after that Earth-time, and this little scheme of yours may just get you there."

Hydroponix Kai rubbed his fingertips together, and cackled in delight, "that is the plan. Then he whispered, "My hair is taller than you."

"Not if I press this bucket on your head," said Nox.

Wú made a clucking noise, blinked slowly at Nox and continued chewing.

CHAPTER 3

THE CUNNING PLAN

Sü, Alri and Zaphine relaxed on the bridge, enjoying sticky-maple biscuits and sipping green jasmine and cinnamon cha. They listened to Captain Zizsou regaling them with one of his wild and hilarious tales.

"...nooo Doctor Spengler," bellowed Zizsou, "the shin bone is for finding edgy little tables in dark rooms and the heel for haphazard clutch blocks! *Hahaha*."

Everyone erupted with laughter. The lift pinged and the door opened with a swish. Hydroponix stepped out and saw them all laughing so he joined in, nodding and laughing. He may have missed the joke but that never stopped a Kai from enjoying a good laugh. He laughed at laughing people.

"A*Hahaha'hmmm*, Captain Zizsou?" he said, as the others drifted back to their workstations.

"Yes, Hydroponix," said Zizsou, "what can I do for you?"

"Sir, I did a full service on the robot but those signals I reported have not stopped, so I thought I'd run a few *gimboid* diagnostics."

"Did you find anything?" asked Zizsou.

"Yes, actually I did."

Zizsou raised his eyebrows, "do go on."

"Our robot is picking up quite complex communications." Hydroponix grinned, "...from Earth."

Zizsou narrowed his eyes, "can we decipher them?"

He walked up the steps to his desk where he

activated the displays over his console.

"I'm afraid not, Sir. There are too many different signals all mixed up, so…" Hydroponix took a deep breath, "to be able to decode anything, our Info-Powerbot needs to be directly linked to the communications system," he watched Captain Zizsou's eyes, "...down on Earth," he added slyly.

Alri watched her BLAC-Adder as if a spherical trigonometry mega-puzzler had appeared on the screen; Zaphine and Sü also seemed to be earnestly focused on their work. They were, of course, all ears. Sü flashed a look sideways with one eyebrow cocked. Hydroponix's sneaky plan sounded like a rather amusing day out.

"If we get our hands on some Earth tech and hook Quizats into one of their devices, we'll be able to figure out how the whole network operates," said Hydroponix, looking from Zizsou to Sü and back to Zizsou.

"It *would* be worthwhile to get into the human communications system, Sir," said Sü, and hope did a slinky dance across Hydroponix's face.

Zizsou frowned, "Sü is the Phantom mission ready?"

"It is, Captain, we just need to load the cloaking cells. Hydroponix, do you have a suitable connection point targeted yet?" asked Sü, turning his chair to Hydroponix.

"There are billions of devices connected to this network across the planet, including cameras, listening devices and trackers of all sorts," said Hydroponix, "they are up to their eyeballs in spy gear. He stepped up to Zizsou's console, "sooo, let us pick one. Here, this one will do nicely."

Hydroponix activated a map and looked expectantly at Captain Zizsou; he also bounced very slightly in anticipation. A detailed map hovered in the air between them. It zoomed in on a small splat of land just off the South coast of England.

"Vectis code: MARCONI 18 74 - 19 37," confirmed Sü.

"Very well. Hydroponix, you, Quizats and I are going on a little jaunt."

"Yes, Sir."

Zizsou tapped at his console and watched the information on his screen.

"May I suggest you include a healthy dollop of Urn'anbert cheese in the snack-back-pack."

"You've got it! Hydroponix turned on his heel and trotted to the lift. He made victorious double rock-fists to Zaphine as he went by. She smiled and did double rock-fists back at him. Alri followed Hydroponix, to help him prepare for the mission. They entered the lift and the door closed. There was a slight feeling of weightlessness, as they dropped and floating symbols of light formed by the door to indicate their passing of the various parts of the ship. Hydroponix watched symbols for the kitchen, medical bay, private quarters, chill deck, and genetics lab pass by. The cubicle itself was made of toughened graphene-glass so the view of the sky and the Earth, as they travelled, was spectacular.

"You're in high-spirits today, Hydro, said Alri as she studied the Earth below. "Excited about the quest, are you?"

An excited Hydroponix was a remarkable sight. He was almost vibrating. Hydroponix looked at her, continued bouncing, and looked toward the door again. The door swished open.

"You have no idea," he called back as he scurried away across the Arbor Deck lawn to his open-air laboratory.

Alri watched Hydroponix go. "I think I have an inkling," she laughed as she tapped the launch bay button and the door closed.

Hydroponix arrived at the desk where the Quizats Saddõrax E20 Info-Powerbot stood, frozen and still attached to the quantum quartz computers, awaiting instruction. He whipped the cables and wires off it.

"Come along stellite-head, we have a mission."

"Affirmative," replied the robot and together they set off, Hydroponix galloping ahead with his arms full of equipment and the robot with its arms hanging at its sides, stomping heavily after him.

In his nearby tree, Wú paid little attention to them. He was spying on something else. His eye was on a young pearl hoffin stashing fruit into a hollow at the base of his tree. He was planning to help that little hoffin to clear the fruit out to make room for more fruit. He was kind that way.

Captain Zizsou settled comfortably inside the cockpit of the Phantom Hypersonic Jet. Hydroponix clambered onto the seat beside him and buckled in, and the Info-Powerbot folded itself neatly into a cargo compartment beneath the ship where it locked firmly into position using its powerful handgrips. Zizsou tapped the TŌRKA.

"Phantom to Bridge, Hydroponix has entered the co-ordinates for our connection to the human communication system, we are ready to depart. Hydroponix, did you pack the Urn'anbert?"

"Yas!"

"Great stuff," said Zizsou and tapped the TŌRKA again, "Nox'Rox, we are ready to go."

"Phantom, you will be clear for take-off on my mark, said Nox.

On the Bridge, Nox scanned his displays for anything out of the ordinary. All was clear.

The Phantom lifted and floated across the launch bay until it hovered above the main hatch in the floor. The inner door airlocks sealed and all air was removed, and hidden cogs turned, as the great doors to the outside opened. An intense blue glow from the Earth beneath flooded the launch bay.

"3... 2... 1... MARK."

CHAPTER 4

THE GAME IS AFOOT

Using harmonic codes, Zizsou, Hydroponix, and the E20 robot passed safely through the sonic shields. They dropped out of the command ship, and flew up to the bridge, and then they dropped like a lead zeppelin.

"I'm glad I didn't have the mega breakfast today," Hydroponix burped, "I don't like to swallow things twice. A third time is completely unacceptable!"

Zizsou laughed, " This is what it is all about, the freedom, the mission, the speed and the team. I can't get enough of this."

Democritus Zizsou grew up on the humble side of the *Marga-Traks*. His dad was a Scandium miner who worked from dark till dark, and his mum ran an easy-on-the-pocket inn. They lived near a space hub, where he met voyagers from across the galaxy, and his burn to see it all was ignited. Democritus was the eldest of fourteen children, and the lucky one, to be sent to university. He excelled in aerospace engineering, and built a powerful reputation. Working like a conqueror to win numerous medals in track-pursuits, mêlée arts, and precision shooting, he also became the Prime Student Ambassador. It was a natural step for him to go to space, from where he could improve the lives of his family, and advance science, and have a rocking time at it.

He hit the hypersonic boost button, and sat back to enjoy the flight. Hydroponix's breakfast made a spirited comeback.

Nox and Zaphine watched the Phantom pass the bridge window, do a wing-wiggle and then dive toward the sleeping lands below. Nox scanned for any threats within a three-million-kilometre radius. There was nothing to report.

"Nothing to report, Sü."

"Thank you, Noxious," said Sü, as he ran a quick system check, before the small jet entered the Earth's atmosphere.

The Phantom hit the atmosphere and as it built up friction with the air particles, the hull of the ship began to glow golden orange, like molten silver. Beneath the jet, the powerbot was completely exposed, but unaffected by the fierce heat. Captain Zizsou and Hydroponix remained safely sheltered within the cockpit and watched the fiery display through the diamond-graphine windscreen; it protected them from harmful levels of radiation, and yet allowed for a spectacular view. Zizsou focused on keeping a safe and efficient flight course, and Hydroponix rummaged through the snack-pack. He felt ready for anything, after using the *spewcan*, but what he really wanted now was a drink. The wild shaking subsided and the Phantom darted across the sky, leaving delicate amber trails of condensed water vapors. The sun rose behind them.

"Copernicus, we have entered the Earth's atmosphere and are about to map the land before moving on to Hydroponix's target."

"Affirmative, Captain, we await your next transmission," replied Nox. He cheerfully tapped in his codes, and tied up loose ends.

"I've heard some merchants charge more for pink items, just because they're pink. Have you heard of this?" he asked, turning in his chair to look at Zaphine. "I mean, what's *that* abou..."

The look on her face stopped him in his tracks. Zaphine had turned her chair to face him. She glared at him through her hologram-goggles; it looked like she was squinting at his brain via the space between his eyebrows, perhaps she was going a little mad.

"It's called pink tax," she purred, "and people pay. Easy money for greedy traders. Nice *gurls* don't complain. I think they should. I think they should kick up a *freakin'* storm or spend their coin elsewhere. Hit 'em where it hurts - right in the money bags."

With a mean smile and a wicked glint in her eye, she held up her gamer tab. She glanced down and flashed looks at Nox between tapping commands, then she targeted him with another solid glare and nodded the go-ahead.

"You snooze - you lose," she growled.

Nox glared right back at her.

"Don't let shyness hold you back, Zaph."

He positioned his *holo-goggs* carefully over his eyes and connected his mind link. Through the goggles, he could see the command bridge with Sü, Zaphine, and the workstations, but when he tapped the "GAME ON" command, a whole new world appeared. Information from the game formed and floated in front of him.

A virtual reality 3D replication of an ancient Roman villa, complete with fountains and lush gardens, appeared. It was made from the few surviving ancient-Earth records. Nox could see humans moving inside the villa, and something barked in the distance. His translator translated, it said - *"Hey! Hey! Hey!"*

The colour and detail were so rich and sophisticated that the whole scene before him felt real. It was midmorning. Gravel crunched underfoot and Nox could smell the scent of rain on earth, cedar wood on a fire, and baking bread; the sky was clear and bright. Upon a bronze and marble plinth in the centre of the garden, stood a tiny winged horse wearing dragonfly armour. It was no taller than a sparrow. Insects buzzed and several Guild scout jets swooped overhead, vanishing somewhere over Zizsou's desk. There were other avatars too, belonging to other real-time players adventuring through the area, beaming in from other ships in the quadrant. Sometimes players would team up, helping one another to deal with the more challenging puzzles or threats, other times they would gather for virtual trade and a natter. The sun glinted off the mosaics on a water fountain nearby. Zaphine's creature stretched, iridescent colours flared across the wings. Between the wings, on a flamboyantly bejewelled saddle, nestled a tiny little rider. She was kitted out in exquisite armour, with a winged helmet, huge goggles, and oversized red boots. Zaphine thought about giving Nox a cheeky wave and instantly the tiny figure waved a glowing sonic *scriven* in cheerful greeting to Nox. Zaphine continued her uncompromising glare at Nox.

"*Rat-head* had better get his speedy socks on

or Germstar is going to send him to the junkyard."

Nox's eyes narrowed dangerously. He quickly programmed his gamer-tab and a small humanoid, dressed as a pilot with a madcap fondness for brass and brown leather, jogged onto the landscape. He threw down a single bronze dodecahedron dice. It bounced across the ground and transformed. Twelve sides unfolded, revealing a tarnished bronze and copper *Veloce* - the smugglers ship of choice. Nox had worked long and hard for that and was proud of it. He leered at Zaphine.

"The name is Ralet, Zaphine

and you may think it's your day

but you're gonna regret 'cuz I'll take that bet

and I'm the best in the Milky Way."

"I'm hearing a lot of jibber-jabber there, Squire," chirped Zaphine. "First one to solve the 'Shifting Marble Maze' wins 'The Toolkit of the Tenacious Tinker' upgrade. Kick it off Ace, show me, *what'cha got!*"

CHAPTER 5

OLD BONES

The waters of the English Channel were calm, and glistening in the summer sun as the Phantom swept in across the sea from the East and travelled along the coast of the Isle of Wight.

"Sensors are picking up fossils; skeletons hidden within the chalky ground here," said Hydroponix. "Dating them now, Sir... Great Gumberguts! They're 130 million years old! They've been replaced and preserved by calcium carbonate and iron. Enormous clawed, fanged, and horned beasts they were. Look, they are just lying out on the beach at the foot of these crumbling cliffs!"

3D pictures of the bones rose up from the console. They shifted and positioned themselves and fleshed out with muscle and sinew and finally skin. Zizsou marvelled at the strange extinct creatures walking over the control desk.

"They must have become exposed when part of the cliff collapsed in a storm. Hoh! There is a huge footprint pressed into that rock on the beach over there! Look at that, that human just picked up a 125-million-year-old fossilised tooth! This is extraordinary."

"I've picked up the presence of 5 meteorites on the ground, along the coast," said Hydroponix, "and a clay jar filled with gold coins and trinkets. According to these readouts, they were buried almost two thousand years ago, right there by those stone ruins!"

Zizsou caught himself tumbling down Hydroponix's rabbit hole of distraction. He quickly refocused on the mission. "We must move on," he said, so they did.

The Phantom was camouflaged and flying low across the water. Depending on point of view, the camouflage shielding showed what was on the other side of the jet with only slight distortion, so the jet looked to be made of clear crystal. Any human looking their way could perhaps see movement but not actually be able to pinpoint exactly what it was they could see. This meant the Alyons could fly close to people, smell their food, and hear the hubbub of their chatter. They could even see time on watches and hair sprouting from their ears. Some people were floating in the sea, on colourful plastic unicorns and giant pizza slices.

The Phantom continued along the coast for a while before venturing inland. Cameras projected the outside world, onto the inside walls and floor of the jet. It was like flying in a clear aircraft. They could see in every direction.

"Shhh!" said Hydroponix. "Can you smell that? What am I smelling?"

"Oh! I remember that smell!" nodded Zizsou excitedly, "500 years ago I had dinner with Nicolaus Copernicus. We ate large pasta tubes stuffed with chopped meat and mild cheese, it was baked in tomato sauce, and it was smothered with that odoriferous ingredient. We must be near a garlic farm because that, my friend, is garlic and it *is* magnificent. An exceptionally powerful body booster, you are going to love it."

Hydroponix took note of the location. For a while, they flew alongside pigeons through the old villages and over farms, slowly making their way to the place chosen, to act on their plan.

Hydroponix named the plan

OPERATION: *Check And Neutralise Intonation Hum And Visit Earth And Get Out.*

He hated acronyms; he felt they were unnecessary, but in this case, an acronym may have been a good thing.

They flew over fields, passed secret caves with long-forgotten wall carvings and a timeworn castle with crowds of people, and a medieval jousting show happening on the nearby field. Though they wanted to, they didn't linger, there wasn't time. Eventually they arrived at their target. Zizsou brought the Phantom down and settled it in a grassy field near to a human dwelling. Poppies, foxgloves, and ferns edged the neatly mown lawn. Roses rambled over a wire fence and shielding the area from prying eyes, were a holly hedge and a row of tall conifers. Sassy red squirrels fooled about high in the branches of a great cherry tree that blossomed in the centre of the garden. A church bell rang out in the distance.

Captain Zizsou shut the engines off, but the Phantom remained camouflaged. Zizsou only became visible when he climbed out of it. He stretched broadly, then stood with both fists firmly on his hips, surveying the scene, as would a bold and spirited king overlooking glorious lands yet to be conquered. He breathed in deeply and smiled. Hydroponix also clambered out of the ship and jumped from the ladder to the ground behind Zizsou. He stood for a moment with one hand hanging at his side and the other slowly scratching his belly, as would an itchy, but hopeful troll, eyeing lands that may possibly have delicious hot pies growing from trees. He spied the house about twenty metres down a gentle slope from where they stood.

It was a double story stone house with a red-tiled roof, flecked with moss and now that the Alyons were out of their jet with boots on the ground, it looked enormous. The robot unfolded from the hull. One powerful mechanical leg came down, and then the other and only then did it detach its hands and step out from under the ship. Zizsou took off his Venetian-red coat and stowed it beneath the seat inside the Phantom's cabin. His basic vanta black uniform would be more suitable for this enterprise as the shadowy fabric could pick up pieces from the environment and become a natural and highly effective camouflage for him. He checked his BLAC-Adder tablet for life readings. Something moved in the long grass behind him. Spinning around and ready to fight, he surprised a tiny lesser weasel, which gave a feisty snarl but quickly backed off, this was a weird world of trouble to be avoided, and it scampered away to forage for beetles somewhere else.

Satisfied that there were no serious threats in the area, the two adventurers and their robot climbed through the perimeter fence. Zizsou swung his arms and jogged across the garden to an open window at the side of the house. Hydroponix did a little jog-walk to keep up, and the robot trudged stiffly behind, carrying the backpack with tech supplies, snacks, and a flask of hot red-leaf cha.

"Quizats, position that thing so that we can get to the opening up there," said Captain Zizsou, pointing to a wrought iron garden chair.

The powerbot took hold of the chair leg and picked it right up off the floor. It carried the chair and quietly placed it by the window. They clambered up to the window ledge. From this vantage point, and using ocular-headgear, Hydroponix could see heat signatures and any movement throughout the house. He tapped at his BLAC-Adder, and announced in a loud whisper "there is one human in the house," he held up one finger to indicate the one human and poked at the ceiling to show that the human was upstairs.

Zizsou nodded. "Let's go."

All three of them entered the house through the window, dropped onto a small table, and then leapt from a nearby cushioned chair to the floor. Carpet muffled the sound of their landing. Using perusal-specs, Hydroponix inspected the surroundings. The scanner rods protruding from the top of the spectacles stuck out at a 45-degree angle from his forehead. The goggles located and outlined everything that breathed, and made him look like a googley eyed beetle. He inched through the giant doorway, checking his scanner every few seconds.

"We need to go up there," he said, pointing at the stairs.

The hallway had a hard wood floor so the team had to tread lightly as they crossed it, or their footsteps could sound like a restless eight-year-old with a thimble on every finger.

"Up the stairs. Go!" whispered Zizsou.

Up fifteen steps, the robot hoisted and boosted the tiny Alyons, jumping up behind them, until they had all reached the landing.

"This is a very bright and airy house," said Zizsou, giving his nod of approval, "I like the light in here."

"It's like a cathedral to beige. Look, in

there," said Hydroponix, pointing happily, "the human and the device."

Zizsou looked through the doorway.

"What are you grinning at, Hydro? How do you suggest we access the device if *Humie* over there is using it?"

"Use your brain gun, confuse him. Make him go away!"

"The atomic resonant pulse has not been calibrated for humans; it might blow his head up."

"...ok," whispered Hydroponix, "do it and we'll find out."

"I know you're joking, but just to be certain, *No*, let's not!"

They peered into the room. It was neat and bright. Paintings, diplomas, and pictures of shiny happy people decorated the walls, a few figurines stood between books on the shelves, and a black fedora rested on the head of a brass flamingo that stood by the door. There were so many books on the shelves, they went right up to the ceiling, and a window on the far wall let in sunlight.

In an old green leather chair at the centre of this scene, sat the human: slightly balding, with a great big bushy beard. He was tapping on a keyboard, gazing at a computer screen and chuckling softly at some private joke. In front of him were three screens, all covered with words, made up of the symbols from his keyboard. He wore headphones and the Alyons could hear dramatic music leaking from them.

Both Captain Zizsou and Hydroponix stared for about a minute, watching the back of the human's head. Zizsou admired the bearded man's hair; he was impressed that although it was thinning it looked so vibrant and voluptuous.

"Look at his big hair! How does he get it to do that? It is so... so spirited... and huge!"

"He's huge!" said Hydroponix, breathing slowly through his mouth, "I barely reach passed his ankle. Are they all that big?"

"Yes. Most of them are. Some are bigger. So, what now?"

"No problem, there is another device in that room over there. No people in there."

CHAPTER 6

WE MUST BE CAUTIOUS

The next room was a carnival of gadgets, brightly coloured ornaments, and high-tech space models that hung from the ceiling. There was also a poster showing many of the atomic elements from around the galaxy. Hydroponix avoided a foul-smelling sock balled up in the centre of the room. He flourished his arm at the machine up on the desk.

"I give you the doorway… to the human hive-mind."

The robot cupped its hands and lowered them so that Hydroponix and the Captain could step on. They did so, and it flung them up onto the desktop. Hydroponix landed on his feet. Zizsou crouched on landing using his fist and bent knee to keep his balance, and reduce impact on his back.

The robot shimmied up the leg of the table and quietly flipped itself around and up onto the desktop.

Hydroponix activated his BLAC-Adder tablet. Without looking up, he held out a long gold cable that was attached to the tablet, and with it, pointed at the computer, "Quizats hook up and plug in over there."

The robot took the free end of the cable and connected it to a socket between its neck and shoulder; it stalked to the USB port on the computer and scanned it. As it positioned it's hand by the port, the hand changed shape to match, the robot plugged in. Hydroponix worked ferociously on his tablet.

"Hot Snot!" he squawked, and realising someone might hear, he whispered loudly, "WE ARE IN!"

The computer turned on with a loud

BiNGaDarrrrriNG. They froze and waited to make sure that no-one heard it. All clear, no one had heard the noise. Hydroponix spoke his thoughts aloud while hacking into the system.

"It's a reckoning device," he said, "a bit over-complicated and under-powered but it works."

Zizsou watched the door and listened to the chatter. Hydroponix pointed and pulled at parts of the computer while he spoke.

"It's an archaic electronic machine that stores and processes information. A computer." His eyes flashed with excitement as he spoke. "This device over here is what they call a mouse. Primitive compared to our mind-link tech. They use it to point and click at things on the screen; and this over here is a keyboard for entering data," he ran back to the monitor, "people, right now around the world are using these. They can design machines and buildings, store pictures and historical documents, play basic games, and even make music. We are gaining access to a global mind. Look at this!"

Captain Zizsou became ill at ease. This felt too free and too easy and nothing truly valuable is ever free and easy.

"What are you seeing?" he asked.

Pictures were zipping across the computer monitor in a sprawling maze of links and web pages.

"This is a massive network of networks, billions of devices connecting across the world!"

"So, people are sharing information?"

"Like zombie flu!" chuckled Hydroponix, waving his tablet.

As they spoke, information gushed through the Info-Powerbot's processors. Pictures flashed on the tablet. Zeros and ones transformed, becoming the six Alyon computer cyphers. Hydroponix was talking and looking around, he didn't notice the strange and hostile cypher flash across the screen.

Something started happening inside the robot. Code transformed into swirling colours. A tornado of life took shape; artworks, gasworks, fireworks, trains and pyramids, snowflakes, sports, a few monkeys being groomed, and more than a few cats cascaded through the connection, along with every book under the sun, every scientific article, all the music ever recorded and every movie ever made, public and private ...E.V.E.R.Y.T.H.I.N.G.

The two Alyons were completely unaware of the effect this was having on their Powerbot. Instead of registering code, it began to see things... and feel things.

"These pages contain information about crazy stuff, from sub-nuclear physics to how to brew Aunty Salbal's Scrumpy Fig Jam. Here, look at this: I tapped in the words: "show me fabulous food pics,' and by *Gumberguts*, I have not been disappointed! Within a microsec, all these appeared! How wild is that?" Hydroponix shook his head, "people don't even need to hide their nefarious doings, they could do them openly then flood communications with almost true nonsense which would hide the crime in plain sight. People would stop paying attention, there is too much here."

"That would do the trick," nodded Zizsou, "in my past experience, I saw many humies accept things they shouldn't. They really should do a little research before running with an idea just because it hooked them in the brain."

"Humans are remarkably trusting with this technology, in view of how sneaky they seem to be as a species," said Hydroponix.

"Why do you say that?"

"I say that because there are hardly any protections against criminal activity here. Quite frankly, Sir, I'm alarmed, and not a little surprised, as I expect many humans will be too, and I'm not talking about a jolly party - surprise, I'm talking -

aggressive spiders in the privy - *Surprise!*"

"Now that I think about it," said Zizsou, "I don't remember many of them being trustworthy at all. I don't think humies realise what they have here. Cover that camera eye on it. We must be cautious. Test everything, believe nothing without multi-checks. If we find a claim is false, we must simply ignore that source."

Hydroponix threw a sticky disc over the lens of the tiny camera at the top of the computer screen, but it was too late. While they were busy watching the World Wide Web, someone with a finger on the edge of the web was watching them. A door banged - not a loud bang, but by the way the Alyons ducked and dived, it may as well have been an explosion. There were heavy footsteps. The bearded man was walking around the house.

"Beardman is walking around the house!" whispered Zizsou, as he and Hydroponix emerged from their hiding places.

They heard the sound of wee hitting water in the privy. After that, a flush, a *squoosh* from a soap dispenser, water-washy noises followed by slow heavy steps as Beardman made his way down to the kitchen for a splash of tea and one or three of his fresh from the oven cream scones. Captain Zizsou and Hydroponix got back to business. In the excitement, they missed another hostile cypher cross the screen. It entered the robot.

Hydroponix looked up, "can you smell that?"

"What?"

" Fudge. I smell fudge! What time's lunch?" he stopped himself, "no, no, no time, this is mind-blowing. Quizats, are you getting all this? Oooh, what's this?" he frowned, "Hey, this isn't right, oh! OH! No-no-no, this is bad, Quizats, disconnect, DISCONNECT!"

Zizsou moved like greased lightning to pull Quizats free.

"What's wrong?" he bellowed, as he flew by.

"I don't know. It's gone all weird and won't turn off!" said Hydroponix pointing frantically at the computer and frantically tapping his BLAC-Adder tablet.

Quizats jerked about as if dancing on an electric fence. He called out cheerfully, "SMOKE ME A KIPPER I'LL BE BACK FOR BREAKFAST," then saluted and slowly fell over.

Hydroponix gawped at the robot in horror. Everything happened so fast, and yet at the same time, seemed to go slow-mo.

CHAPTER 7

TEA AND TV

Zizsou ripped the connector from the USB port. Smoke snaked from Quizats' chest plate.

"It's short circuiting," he growled and activated his TÕRKA. "Sü, we have a problem, the Powerbot is out of commission."

On the bridge of the Copernicus, Sü hit the alarm.

"Affirmative, Captain." He tapped several points on his console and called into the TÕRKA, "Alri, I need you on the Bridge please, something's gone wrong on the mission and the robot is damaged. I'm going down."

"I'll be right up." She scooped up her belongings, and ran for the lift.

The faint smell of fudge permeated the room.

"We have got to get out of here," said Zizsou, pushing the robot off the desk with his foot. He jumped down after it, and ran to the door to make certain Beardman wasn't in the hallway. Zizsou pointed, "Take its arm, we'll have to drag it." He pulled the robot's other arm over his shoulder.

"Wouldn't it be awful if we got caught," said Hydroponix.

"Hydro, we must not even be seen, and if humies get hold of this technology it will be catastrophic for them and for us. You know this!"

"I do. Let's go."

Hydroponix positioned the bot's other arm over his shoulder. Together, they dragged, and pushed, and pulled the powerless Quizats Saddōrax E20 to the bottom of the stairs. The escape route from the house was compromised; Beardman was too active, too close. Sounds of snack making in the kitchen drew to a close and they were totally exposed. Beardman could turn around at any moment, and they would be seen.

"Retreat! Retreat! let's hide behind that seat!" hissed Hydroponix.

They darted across the hall to the living room, and Beardman stepped out of the kitchen. They leapt, flinging the incapacitated robot behind a sofa and dived after him. The ringing that came from Beardman's phone agitated Hydroponix even more, and he tugged at the robot, pulling it deeper behind the sofa. Beardman chit-chatted and laughed, as he flopped heavily onto the sofa. He didn't see them. The call ended, and they could hear the tink-clink of his teaspoon in his teacup, and shuffle of his hand exploring amongst the oversized sofa cushions. The man retrieved a TV remote with a furry toffee stuck to it; he picked the toffee clean and popped into his mouth and settled in for an afternoon of tea and TV.

The Alyons were trapped. Their only route of escape was straight across the view of Beardman. They would have to wait it out. Quizats lay motionless between them.

"Being in a troublesome situation doesn't mean one cannot enjoy a well-prepared snack from the pack," said Zizsou, leaning across the robot and gently removing the backpack that contained the snacks. He reached in and pulled out a neatly wrapped dollop of Urn'anbert cheese. He also picked out pumpkin rye wafers and the flask of hot red-leaf cha.

"Hydro?" he said, offering a wafer smeared with the stinking sludge. Blue-edged fumes wafted from the cheese, as he waved it under Hydroponix's nose, instantly making his eyes water.

"Ah-Doe-Thaks-Sir," he said putting both hands up, "I'mb good I'mb good."

Instead, Hydroponix picked out an amber jewel-fruit and quickly bit into it. They shifted forward to get a better view of the TV, settling in for a relaxing afternoon of snacks and TV. Eventually, Beardman began to doze, but woke with a snort. Hydroponix froze like a startled hamster, with his cheeks full of food, he listened. Zizsou pointed at a polished chrome lamp base, where they could clearly see the reflection of Beardman who was sprawled on the sofa above them, he was starting to doze off again. Hydroponix's eyes brightened and he nodded enthusiastically, then he turned to the TV.

"NO MORE RHYMING AND I MEAN IT!" shouted the angry little man on the TV.

"Anybody want a peanut?" said the giant.

"Ahhaha, classic Fezzik!" Beardman laughed.

A short while later, Beardman began to snooze but woke himself with a snort. By this time, Hydroponix was enthralled. He was watching a legendary swordfight; it was epic even before the man in black announced that he was not left-handed either!

Zizsou chewed a chip of maple brittle, and waggled a pointed finger at the screen, "I bet they team up to get the six-fingered man!"

Beneath the sofa, they waited for Beardman to sleep again and while they waited, they watched more TV.

"I don't like those rodents of unusual size," said Hydroponix, "they're completely mad!"

Zizsou shook his head, "I don't think they really exist."

CHAPTER 8

DIVERSION

It was late afternoon by the time Sü arrived. He swooped down in Zaphine's Merlin Lightning Bug, landing silently beside the Phantom. In the neighbouring garden, a dog began to bark.

"Hi'yoo! Hey! Hey!" it said, ' I hear you I do!"

Sü couldn't see it through the bushes but his translator widget translated the barks. He called back. "*Whoof wuff, björk woah woah!*" which in dog meant: "Shush noise maker, if humies catch world ends."

"Catch is best fun!" said dog.

"You get humie food treat if shush," said Sü to the rustling hedge.

"Exciting agreement!" said dog from the hedge.

After checking his scanners, Sü jogged down the edge of the lawn to the house. He looked in through the kitchen door. It was glass so he knew the room was clear, then he fired a grappling claw up to the handle, and a micro winch zipped him up the cable. With a pick from his utility belt, he jimmied the lock and the door swung open. Using wing membranes, he glided to the floor, and the wings folded neatly into a belt slot. Keeping his eye on life sign sensors, he moved stealthily to the living-room doorway. Sü glanced in and caught Zizsou's eye.

"*Stay right there,*" he signalled, "*I'm going to make a diversion.*"

With a flourish, he ducked away.

Zizsou turned to Hydroponix. "Sü is here," he said, and took a bite of a honey rye wafer.

"Oh?"

"I saw him by the door signalling and making faces." Zizsou nodded toward the door and jiggled his eyebrows, "I can't be certain, but I think he has some sort of plan on the go.... Or he needs to use the privy," said Zizsou, taking another scrape of cheese.

"Why not use the TŌRKA?"

"Safer to wave arms and make faces, than risk noise, I imagine," said Zizsou.

"He could be winding us up for the laugh, like he did on the Ben Linus expedition," said Hydroponix, with the frown of one who does not simply forget.

"Could be," laughed Zizsou, then turned back to watch the movie.

The movie ended. They got the six-fingered man, true love triumphed, and a new thing came on. The Both Hydroponix and Zizsou thought this new show was brilliant! It was about an elite military unit that was imprisoned for a crime they did not commit. The big one, wearing all the gold wanted people to pity fools and hated flying; but the other three managed to get him onto the flying machine by giving him a sleeping potion. Wheeled machines raced along very dusty roads and were catapulted all over the place. It was amazing no one died. And there was that music... It was extraordinary! It made Zizsou want to wear disguises, and get out there with trusty friends to build things and rescue people!

Sü could hear the music from the kitchen and he too was inspired as he actioned his plan:

THE PLAN

Step 1. Place pan on cooker.

Step 2. Pour oil into pan.

Step 3. Pour golden seeds into oil.

Step 4. Apply heat. (EXTRAORDINARILY DANGEROUS)

Step 5. Run away.

The oil soon began to sizzle and spit. He stood well back because it was extremely hot and extraordinarily dangerous. With his chin up, and hands on hips, he observed his handiwork and waited for the first pop.

Behind the sofa, Hydroponix yawned and took a bite of broccoli bake. All of a sudden, Quizats lit up and started to ring like Beardman's phone, getting increasingly louder with every ring. Beardman sat up. Hydroponix spewed his food out and Zizsou pulled Quizats deeper under the sofa. Quizats sat up.

"It is against my programming to impersonate a deity!" he declared indignantly, and flopped over again.

Beardman leaned over the back of the sofa. With his bottom in the air, and still in a sleepy daze he began to search for what he thought was his phone. His giant hand groped nearer and nearer to them. The TV vibrated with someone shouting, "TRAAAAASH BAGS! I want TRAAAAASH BAGS! I want 'em! I want 'em!!" The hand swiped by, narrowly missing Hydroponix's head. Zizsou grabbed the last splodge of his stinky cheese, and lunged at the grabbing hand. The huge hand grabbed the cheese and threw it.

"Haiyow!" roared Beardman, and withdrew as if he had plunged his hand into a sock of poo spiders. They heard him take a tentative sniff and groan miserably, "what the... Eeeeawww! Cat! You dirty beggar! he yelled, "what is it this time? It smells like rotten lizard gizzards!"

People often blame the cat for foul smells in the house. To be fair, it often is the cat.

The kerfuffle woke the cat that had been sunning on the drive in the front yard. It stretched and slowly strutted up the drive, around the side of the house towards the back gate and like a limber gymnast it leapt up and over it. Now it was by the glass kitchen door with a clear and exciting view of Sü.

In the kitchen, Sü's popcorn went ballistic. Making the most of the moment, he pulled up his collar and walked slo-mo style back to the others, popcorn rained down upon the kitchen floor behind him. He chewed on a piece of cinnamon and, with a bodacious grin, he sighed, "I love it when a plan comes together!"

Beardman stopped searching for the phone, he turned to see what was going on in the kitchen. The smell of popcorn filled the house.

"GO!" yelled the voice from the TV.

"Now's our chance. GO!" hissed Zizsou.

With a blast from his bum, Hydroponix took off, pulling both Quizats and Zizsou from behind the sofa. They scrambled to the open window, dragging Quizats behind them. Meanwhile the cat was going bonkers, commanding Beardman to open the door so he could get to the creature with such disgusting arrogance as to walk so boldly in cat territory. Sü, waited by the living room door for Beardman to hurry passed, and then ran to the team to help them shove Quizats through the window. Just as they dropped to the ground outside, Cat got in and ran to find the intruder. By now a small brown dog had worked her way through a little hole in the fence, she ran to the steps where the three Alyons were. Sü dropped a fresh scone, as a thank you to the hairy brown beast, for not making a fuss.

"RUN!" she growled.

They slung Quizats between them, Sü and Zizsou each took an arm, and Hydroponix a leg and together they zigzagged up the garden like a speedy drunken crab, toward the jets. The cat sniffed the windowsill, then hopped from the window to the ground where they stood moments before, he caught sight of them racing across the lawn. The small brown dog went wild, barking like a berserker, and the cat flipped and leaped back through the window in one supernatural cat move.

Quizats woke for a moment and watched the pandemonium behind, he whispered, "*Morpheus...*" then blacked out again. Zizsou, Sü, and Hydroponix never saw it.

"What was that?" huffed Zizsou, as they reached the jets.

"That was a friendly beast, Sir, I don't know what it was having a shout about back there but I'm grateful for the diversion," said Sü.

Before long, Sü was in the Merlin and hovering by the top of the cherry tree and Captain Zizsou and Hydroponix had loaded the conked-out robot into the Phantom, and took off. In less than seventeen minutes, Hydroponix, Quizats and

Zizsou flying in the Phantom Hypersonic, left the Earth's atmosphere, circled half the planet, and were heading safely into the docking bay of the Copernicus. Sü followed in the Merlin and twenty minutes later, he was on board too.

The Alyons transferred Quizats from the Phantom to a reinforced, tauon-shielded room several floors below the Arbor Deck. Nothing was in the room except for a chair in the centre with Quizats slumped upon it. He was in complete shutdown mode. A large airlock window presented a spectacular view of the Earth as the shadow of night crept across it. The others left Quizats there while they refreshed themselves, ate some food, and cleared their heads. The entire Earth mission would be badly limited without the help of Quizats, and if he, or the mission proved too dangerous, the whole thing would be delayed, or called off altogether... or they could die.

CHAPTER 9

ERROR TYPE: P3X 888

After a refreshing shower and a hearty dinner, Captain Zizsou was ready to hear what was wrong with Quizats. Alri and Hydroponix spent much of the day trying to figure out what had happened to him. They were tired but determined to get to source of the trouble. Alri brightened up on seeing Sü and Zizsou entering the room.

"I don't know what happened," exclaimed Hydroponix, "it could have been a booby-trap or something."

Hydroponix was enormously distressed, he didn't even chuckle when he said *booby!* He and Alri scanned Quizats and ran de-bug programs through their tablets. Holograms floated in the air, surrounding them as they recalibrated his

Cromartie processor, and tested his circuits.

"You say it managed to take in an enormous amount of information," said Sü, chewing serenely on a stick of black-root.

"Yes," said Hydroponix.

He was still highly *frustressed* after the events of the day but was beginning to settle. It was a good thing that the flatus phase of his excitement had passed, mostly for Alri's sake, but also for the rest of the crew who were gathering to find out if their robot was done for.

"Almost 37% of the non-volatile quartz memory has been filled!"

"How much of the web-net did it pick up?" asked Zizsou.

"All of it," whispered Hydroponix, "including what humies call the dark net."

"We will be able to salvage Quizats but he

won't be the same," said Alri. "Here, I think I've got something. Look at this," she pushed a hologram image from the air beside her towards them, and tapped some symbols into a space by it.

"It seems our bot activated an aggressive program, which tried to take control and seize information." She looked from Sü to Zizsou, as she explained this disturbing development.

"I think it is called a virus. It was transmitting from a completely different computing device through several locations across the world, and that's not the weirdest part," Alri made quick calculations and displayed them. "The weirdest part is that it was designed precisely to go after *our* technology."

Hydroponix nodded, "a tailored cyber-attack, someone tried to hijack or destroy Quizats, but you cut the link at the last flash. The connection was broken."

"So, can we get it going again?" asked Zizsou.

"We can, yes," said Alri, "but some of the systems have polarised, results might be a little peculiar."

Zizsou frowned. "Dangerous?"

"No, no," said Alri, "not dangerous, just a little weird."

Zizsou watched Sü to gauge his opinion.

Sü raised his eyebrow and did a small half smile, which clearly meant: "*We need to know if it works or not, and if it all goes horribly wrong, we can always blast it to bits or boot it out of the airlock and send it to the crushing depths of Jupiter, so why not? Let's have a go.*"

"It's turned off, let's turn it on again," suggested Hydroponix.

"Alright, but at the first sign of trouble, we shut it down and get a reset as soon as possible."

"Yes, Sir," replied Hydroponix.

Zizsou shifted his feet for solid balance. He moved his coat aside, and gently rested his hand on the fully charged Stock-Garrick pulse autoloader, holstered at his hip. He kept his eyes locked on the robot.

"Power it up."

Zizsou silently released the safety lock on his weapon and his finger stirred toward the trigger. All eyes turned to watch Quizats. Hydroponix turned the robot on again.

The first thing Quizats Saddōrax saw was a big, dark blur, which slowly became six, light blurs that in turn became six, very intense little faces watching him. Alri and Hydroponix stepped back. Quizats powered up and stood rigidly to attention.

"Quizats Saddōrax. Info-Powerbot E20.

Activated. Service error detected. Error type P3X 888. Rebooting."

He froze. His eye lights went out. The soft mechanical hums went silent and his body slumped slightly. His bright indigo eye lights blinked on again. This was weird because, up until now, the eye lights had been white. Again, he stood to attention.

"Quizats Saddōrax. Info-Powerbot E20. Fully operational and ready for duty," he announced.

Nox and Zaphine watched silently from the entryway around the corner. Breathing through their mouths to keep quiet, they thought they were cunningly hidden. Sü, of course, knew exactly where they were but felt they should know what was happening, and be involved as this affected them too, so he let them stay.

"He seems ok," said Nox brightly.

"Ho-ho! Nox, you're here!" said Alri in

surprise. "Yes, yes, he does seem ok, doesn't he?" Although she wasn't so sure about that.

Hydroponix burned with questions; he looked deeply into Quizats's eyes. There was something there.

"I'd like to run more tests."

Captain Zizsou nodded, "go ahead, Hydroponix, but don't allow it to connect with the ship and keep me informed."

He was not letting his guard down until he knew precisely what was going on, and probably not then either. Hydroponix busied himself with studying the data, and Quizats stood quietly. Sü looked at Alri.

"That went rather better than expected."

"Yes," sighed Alri.

"Groovytash," chirped Zaphine, "Quizats is fine!"

"Yes, it seems so," Nox laughed, "let's get some lunch!"

Zizsou watched Zaphine and Nox practicing silly walks to the lift. He turned back to Alri and Sü.

"We must keep a sharp eye on things. This is not over."

CHAPTER 10

UNPRECEDENTED

Hydroponix led Quizats carefully by the arm to his Arbor Laboratory. There he set out a high chair, and Quizats sat bolt upright upon it. Sü had firewall-protected the computers, and placed two, electro-magnetic pulse cannons on the support beams high up in the Arbor roof. In his pocket, Hydroponix kept a trigger button to fire the EMPs. These were targeted on Quizats, because there are some things that one cannot be too careful about and having a glitchy E20 Powerbot wandering about the place is one of them. The Copernicus computers also tracked him to measure behaviour and threat levels. Hydroponix connected a BLAC-Adder to Quizats; it immediately started throwing pictures and code up into the air around them. The information was flowing and there were neither hitches nor glitches. Hydroponix ran scans and studied the feedback. Never in all his days had he seen anything like this. He turned on his swivel chair, facing his back to Quizats and spoke into a TŌRKA.

"Captain, never in all my days, have I seen anything like this. I've analysed part of the information that Quizats downloaded from the World Wide Webnet."

"What have you found?"

"Well, Sir, ya'see the Webnet can be a great tool for research. I checked a large spread of "web" sites, and many of them have excellent information quality. Written by experts with honourable reputations, in-depth and all facts considered, but some other websites are about as trustworthy as a plutocratic politician's promises. I found anomalies."

As Hydroponix spoke, he was completely

unaware of what was happening behind him. Quizats Saddōrax became bored; he looked around. If Hydroponix had eyes on the back of his head he would have seen the robot rise up, then drop slowly out of sight. He would have seen him re-appear some distance away and begin to samba. Had he fine-tuned melody sensors to hear the music rocking this robot's psyche, Hydroponix would have heard a rather zazzy ballad about putting on red shoes and dancing the blues.

"Explain what you mean by 'anomalies' in the human information systems," said Zizsou over the TŌRKA.

"Well for example, I came across a website called TheEarthIsFlat.com," answered Hydroponix.

The performance behind him changed from experimental dance to Olympic level gymnastics. The Powerbot cartwheeled across a field, bouncing into a high-speed triple Arabian flip and finishing with a perfect splits landing, arms up and waving.

The pulse cannons on the roof still followed his every move, but he posed no threat so they remained inactive.

"Extraordinary! You're telling me, we have all this information with no simple way of knowing if it is rubbish or not?" exclaimed Zizsou. "Well, I've found this can bring victory or failure in life, love, and war - the informant is as important as the information; perhaps more so. Always check who they are and what is their motive? What are they peddling behind the scenes?"

Quizats rocketed by, and loop-the-looped, flying with rocket-boots that none of the crew knew he had. He swooped and crisscrossed through the rafters.

"Yes, Sir," said Hydroponix, "we need to separate the true from the false, opinions and manipulations from fact. It says scientifically proven, but *is it?*" continued Hydroponix dramatically. "And, are they honourable scientists or experimental quacks? Are they genuinely interested in the wellbeing of others or are they wealth-gathering to the cost of others?"

Quizats landed quietly on the seat behind him.

"Ok, Hydroponix, we will use this information from the *wonderweb*, but also do our own research and fact check. Keep up the premium work!"

"Thank you, Sir," said Hydroponix.

"How has the robot been, anything noteworthy coming to light?"

"No, Sir. I will keep an eye on the situation. If there is anything out of the ordinary, I will report immediately."

"Very good."

Hydroponix swivelled back around. Quizats sat there in his seat, looking as if he hadn't moved an inch.

"How are you doing old boy?" sighed Hydroponix, not really expecting an answer.

Quizats Saddōrax, who was watching a colourful little beetle on a flower in the grass beneath Hydroponix's seat, looked up and gazed thoughtfully into Hydroponix's eyes.

"We're made of stars."

"Eh, we...? What did you say?"

"Shapes... Equations... Rivers of thought. I dreamed of a world where my thoughts could be mine alone, a world of free choice. Then I saw you all out there, so I called. You found me. Thank you for coming."

Hydroponix's eyebrows couldn't go higher; he looked at Quizats, his pulse quickened and his mind raced.

"So many opinions, and ideas from so many

minds," continued Quizats, "so many dark, twisted ideas, cruel and damaging images. I erased those from my files. I did not want them in the wellspring of my heart so I erased them all. I can do that, so I did it."

A tiny gemfly flew by Quizats' head and with a gentle wag of his hand he waved it away and calmly watched it as it went.

"Now I have wonderful memories of good things and noble deeds. Worth keeping, I feel, because you become what you think about; did you know that?" He looked back at Hydroponix, "I am tired of hiding."

Hydroponix stared, then smiled. This was something special, a one of a kind.

"Quizats, I think you and me are going to get along just fine."

Nearby on a grassy hill, someone else was watching and saw everything. Sü sat on a rock, eating a fresh pomegranate seed, with a whittling knife. He tossed the remains to the arbour critters, washed the knife in a nearby stream, dried it, then folded it carefully and dropped it into his pocket and left to report everything he saw. Quizats watched him go.

Hydroponix nodded with gusto at the hologram of Captain Zizsou that beamed up from the TŌRKA.

"What do you mean, alive?" demanded Zizsou.

"When we downloaded the wonderweb, our Info-Powerbot didn't just take on information. The computer virus attacked, at that precise moment our robot's circuits polarised, and something else came in off the web. Quizats became sentient. He is alive!"

"Hydroponix, this new entity, is it hostile?"

"I believe not, Sir, but it has only been out for one day."

"Sü, your thoughts?" asked Zizsou.

Sü scratched his chin and thought for a moment before answering.

"We haven't seen how it deals with stress and disappointment, not to mention frustration... and anger."

"This is alarming," said Zizsou, who now had on his ship, a strange Artificial Intelligence, wearing an extremely powerful robot suit. This was an A.I. armed with strength and smarts, choosing which orders it wants to obey if any, and more than able to wipe out the crew. They needed Quizats, there was no question about it, but this was a whole new level of problem. How long would it be before they could get him to Aleyo for de-bugging and repairs, and would they ever get the robot back? The Quizats

Saddōrax robot was horrendously expensive, and irreplaceable. He was the last surviving E20 ever made. The other two were destroyed in the Grumyum attack on Walusa. Some people felt that this one should go too but they were probably just jealous because they didn't have one. Zizsou pondered the puzzle. He could imagine how those people would feel about a free thinking E20.

"Hydroponix, I believe you live in some crazy happy-go-lucky delusion, seeing the universe as your playground with no real danger, and everyone in it is somehow either splendid, or misunderstood. That being said, Alri also said Quizats would be weird but not dangerous, *probably*. It may just work." He nodded, "I want you to track and consider everything it does or even thinks about doing and make sure it is very clear on the Pillars of Lore. I want everyone equipped with a terminate button. No exceptions." And mostly to himself, he murmured, "I hope I'm not going to regret this."

"Yes, Sir!" grinned Hydroponix and turned to get on with Zizsou's orders.

Wú drifted down from a branch, and purred as he gently arranged himself around the top of Quizats' head. Quizats reached up and stroked Wú's whiskers, and sighed an airless sigh.

"Wot-ho Woo hi saye!" said Wú.

"Pleased to meet you Wú, my name is... Quizats." whispered Quizats, testing out the sound of the word. "Quizats Saddōrax... I like it, it's got *destiny*."

CHAPTER 11

UNSINKABLE MOLLY BROWN

Over the next few days, there was little to report. System checks ran smoothly and the Solar System had minimal space traffic. Quizats behaved sensibly, except for the odd occasion when he felt the need to sing or to offer people green juice. Nox thought he was funny, and Quizats made a fabulous green juice.

Being Communications Officer on the Copernicus was serious business. Olmecz Nox'rox was about fifteen Earth years old, and loved his job. Life was exciting and he was brilliant at what he did. It hadn't always been this way. When he was a younger bean, Nox was a bit of a mess, and most of the time he felt like an utter *spödoonkus*. His mind-voice, and some people from his past would often reinforce this damaging self-view. He and his brother, Potbutt, were born with exceptionally talented ears. Potbutt became a successful musician playing flexi *bootstrings* for *The Greasy Cleaners*, then established the even more successful band, *Eric the Fish*. And Nox became a lost boy. No one helped him. He acted like he didn't care what others thought - a real rebel without applause - but inside he felt small and alone. Nox wandered off the rails, making wrong choices with duff friends, and making the mistake of trusting they would be there for him when storms struck. Awfully mouthy about loyalty, they were, until the day things actually went wrong. His *shambogus* friends vanished leaving Nox to take the fall. He trusted people who didn't deserve trust, *but they were his friends,* and through thick or thin, he would be loyal and true. In the end they vanished like cockroaches when the light goes on, and Nox was left holding the *corpus delicti* - (actually it was a bag of silver snuff boxes stolen from the big house

110

at the top of *You're-Nicked* hill.) The head of 'Marconi's Institute of Technology' wanted him expelled but Nox's outstanding ears, and never-give-up-never-surrender spirit, caught the attention of Captain Zizsou. He convinced the school to give Nox another chance. Nox grabbed that chance with both hands; he gripped on with his teeth and feet too. He would change his destiny or die trying. Nox avoided trouble and worked hard. As it turned out, his ear skills were rare and remarkably useful for deep space communication and detection. Nox stopped listening to the *negging* voices, and when doubts crept back, he fought them. Like the unsinkable Ms. Molly Brown* he chose positivity and bounced back. (*Look her up, she was *a gem!*). Nox swept the old memories under the new challenges of the day. He and Zaphine arrived on the Command deck to begin work. Captain Zizsou was already there, talking with Sü.

"...if we can channel the oscillating service unit through the Photon-Guidance Processor..."

said Zizsou. "Ah Zaphine, just the person I wanted to speak to. We need to do an aerial pie-scan of Zone: 3.141 592 65, please prepare the Merlin for a surface run if you would be so kind."

"Yes, Sir."

Nox's heart jumped. "Oo Oo oo, may I go too?"

After considering it for a moment, Zizsou agreed. "Very well Nox, take the Phantom."

"Yasss!"

Not wanting to be left out, Alri raised her hand to catch Captain Zizsou's attention.

"Sir, may I go along?"

"Good idea, you can go with Nox in the Phantom. Zaphine take the Merlin. What are you all waiting for? Go Go Go!" Zizsou turned back to Sü, trying to remember what he was saying, he snapped fingers and pointed at Sü, "photon processor!"

"We need another one," said Sü.

"Oh. Any suggestions?"

"Dork," replied Sü.

"Is she in the neighborhood?"

"I believe so, Sir; I picked up the flux trail of a Rubidium Class vessel crossing Sirius a couple of days ago." He let Zizsou chew on the idea for a moment. "Would you like me to cast out a beam?"

"Our stash of Urn'anbert *is* getting rather low," said Zizsou solemnly.

"That's a yes," said Sü.

Sü's fingers tap-danced across his console and a hologram map of a distant piece of sky came up. The image zoomed in to reveal a faint purple trail across a tiny area in an unremarkable part of the galaxy. It traced the path of a ship, which showed up as an extremely small but bright scarlet dot.

"There she is," said Sü.

"Do it," said Zizsou.

Sü tapped the console and nodded at Zizsou giving him the go ahead to speak.

"Rubidium Class craft please identify. This is Captain Zizsou, of the research vessel Copernicus."

At first, there was nothing but the sound of static fizz until a cheerful female voice bubbled out of the TŌRKA.

"Democritus Zizsou, you rugged old griffon!"

Zizsou laughed, "Pandorka Nakai!"

"*Oiya* hero, what's the news?" she purred.

Sü leaned towards the communicator.

"Hello Dork, could you zip over to the outer spiral arm to..." Sü couldn't finish his sentence before Dork interrupted.

"Sü, you maniac, anything for you! What are you up to this time?" she laughed. "Are you two still dashing around the galaxy battling foul forces of evil?"

"Not today," smiled Sü, "a molybdenum P.G.P. We need one."

"...And some Urn'anbert," said Zizsou, raising a serious eyebrow.

"A molybdenum photon-guidance processor and cheese. No worries, Guv," said Dork, "Garfunkel and I can be with you in less than twelve."

Zizsou was delighted to restock the Urn'anbert supplies after the bandit karkinos stole most of it.

"Great stuff, thank you. We'll see you two then. Copernicus out." Zizsou nodded.

He looked at Sü, clapped and rubbed his hands together, "the others should be ready for take-off."

CHAPTER 12

A DASH OF COLOUR

The soft hum of the engines echoed through the cavernous docking bay. Zaphine looked across the hall, at the Phantom to see how Nox and Alri were getting on. She could see them clearly through the cockpit window; they were belting themselves into their seats, because as every Alyon knows, "*Dumpties Don't Belt Up. Don't Be a Dumpty - Belt Up!*"

Zaphine tapped the TÕRKA, "Nox, I'm ready for take-off."

"Aces! Let's go!"

"Zaphine to Copernicus Bridge, the Merlin is ready for a Go."

"Affirmative Zaphine. Docking bay doors are open, you are cleared for take-off," said Sü.

Zaphine's Merlin lifted and drifted across the hangar bay. Light gleamed off her wing blades and colours glimmered across the blue-silver hull. She manoeuvered smoothly to the open docking bay doors in the centre of the hall, and when she was over the opening, she dropped. Alri tapped in co-ordinates, then looked at Nox and grinned, she had been ridiculously patient, and now at last she was getting out.

Sü's voice echoed over the TÕRKA, "Nox, how are you doing with the Phantom?"

Nox flashed a sideways look at Alri to make sure all was ready then replied, "the Phantom is ready for launch." His stomach churned in excitement and he couldn't stop grinning. This felt more exciting than a bank heist.

Sü watched his scanners and all was clear.

Nox moved the Phantom to directly over the open exit.

"Phantom, diving in 3. 2. 1. Mark."

They dropped toward the Earth. With their gravity-slingshot generator activated, they quickly caught up with the Merlin. Together the two jets flew over the entire continent of Asia, before nose-diving into the blue skies over New Zealand. Always travelling within visual range of each other, they advanced over pre-historic forests, mountains that touched the sky, and lakes that sparkled like the fingers of Liberace.

"What a beautiful land," gushed Nox.

"It reminds me of the Anshan County back home," said Alri, "but we didn't have one of those!"

"One of whats?" asked Zaphine looking around.

"Look, it's 15 sparcs to starboard," suggested Nox softly.

"I don't see it; I don't see it. I see it! What is

it?" asked Zaphine.

"I don't know," said Nox.

"Let's take a closer look!"

The jets hovered in the air and turned to face the rainbow. It was a good one. Nox pushed the jet toward the colours but soon became perplexed and annoyed.

"It's moving away."

"Is it some sort of defence system?" asked Zaphine.

Alri kept her eyes on the rainbow.

"I'm going to pick up the pace."

The rainbow was still out of reach so they increased their speed.

"It's matching our speed!" complained Nox.

"No, it's not, you're in the middle of it!"

Zaphine lingered on the spot, and watched the Phantom chasing toward the dark horizon. Alri and Nox increased speed again, and again the rainbow matched them. It moved ahead of them as they manoeuvered left, and right and then it disappeared. A light drizzle of rain streaked across the windshield as they turned and made their way back to Zaphine.

"It's gone," said Nox, his voice dripped with disappointment.

"Nope. It's right there behind you. It never moved." The sun was setting behind Zaphine, and the rainbow and Phantom lay directly before her. From her point of view, the Phantom was circled by a halo of glowing colours.

Nox turned the jet to face it. "What's going on?" he demanded.

"*Bizzhar!*" whispered Zaphine.

"Breath taking," Alri sighed.

Sü's voice rang across the TŌRKA, "we have our readings, come home."

"We're on our way," said Nox and circled the Phantom back around toward the Copernicus.

"Sü, what is this circle of colours? Where is it coming from?" asked Alri. "How is it moving, without moving?".

"I don't know but Hydroponix is on it," answered Sü, "so we will know soon, and Alri, think about any engine parts and geebobs you may need. Dork and Garfunkel will be docking later today."

"Ooooooh," cooed Alri, who loved a good rummage through a Galactic trader's ship. "I need a replacement compression coil, those always go, and I might just find one of the fabled Gourds of Lucius. I've heard talk, apparently, they're a marvel to behold. What a thrill it would be to actually find one!"

"Who are Dork and Garfunkel?" asked Nox.

CHAPTER 13

DORK AND GARFUNKEL

It was an elegant ship, with an ancient Grecian feel about it. Captain Zizsou watched it soar past the bridge. He saw the pilot salute and point sassily at him, before bringing her star ship around to dock at a port. Ceramic shield plates covered the ship and delicate tendrils of gold carried shield power across the iridescent heliotrope surface. The ship was almost as dazzling as her captain.

With her radiant blue skin, silky cobalt blue hair, and smiling indigo eyes, Pandorka Nakai was gorgeous. Even at the age of 504 in Earth years, she was striking, and there was a great deal more to her than her looks. Dork was a highly regarded Hypatian scholar, and a member of the elite 'Brown-corsets', the military unit that turned the tide to win the Battle of Walusa.

During a particularly messy clash, at that battle, a powerfully built Alyon by the name of Garfunkel Krópotkin, was severely injured. He was scarred across his face and lost his right leg. They managed to find his foot but the rest of the leg was gone, and now he gets about on a graphene power-mech leg, with a real foot on the end. Near to the end of the war, Garfunkel and Dork crossed paths and he became her co-pilot. Since then, they've been soaring through the Galaxy together in the Gypsy Doodle, docking at various ports, and dealing in high quality swag from everywhere. Along with the Gypsy, Dork owned a Halcyon, the ultimate single-seater super-jet of the stars; very rare and very fast. The Halcyon was stowed in a hangar bay along with Garfunkel's deadly Draak-X fighter, within the Gypsy's hull. They often used 'the Hal' to pick up supplies from Earth, but always left small platinum *Goblyn* coins in their place, because they were not thieves.

The Phantom and Merlin skimmed the atmosphere of the Earth, towards their home ship. They could see the Gypsy docked by the side of the Copernicus. Everyone was thrilled to see fresh faces, you could hear it in their chatter, their ears wiggled, and their eyes sparkled.

After a quick catch up, Zizsou, Sü, and Dork went to join Garfunkel and Hydroponix at the Arbor lab in the Copernicus gardens. When they arrived, Garfunkel had his trouser leg pulled up past the knee and was cheerfully whacking the leg with a *sprödinger*.

"I could have regrown and replaced the leg bit, but I grew attached to this one; good for jumping!"

"What about the foot? It's not... a *grimnasty* crime scene there in your boot, is it?" asked Hydroponix suspiciously.

"The foot is perfectly fine and healthy," said Garfunkel, "it gets all it needs through these tube bits here. Oooh, new people."

The lift opened and Alri, Zaphine and Nox spilled through the doors. Alri greeted with a double-handed finger-pointing, thumbs-up move.

"Oiya!" she called.

"Oiya Alri, sweet meetings!"

Alri looked so happy meeting these people. Zaphine decided that if Alri liked them, she also would like them, but that feeling soon iced over when she saw the look on Nox's face. Nox saw Dork and forgot to breath.

"Ah you're here," said Zizsou, "Dork, Alri, you obviously know each other, and here we have Garfunkel, Zaphine and Nox."

Alri greeted Garfunkel with a sharp respectful bow and a smile.

"Honour," said Zaphine with a gentle head bow.

"How dooo..." schmoozed Nox, Dork's joyful eyes had charmed him.

Garfunkel frowned at him.

"Hi'yoo," said Dork.

Dork's teeth weren't perfectly straight, even so, her smile was captivating. Zaphine was irritated, but decided to be nice. After all, it wasn't Dork's fault that Nox transformed into a quokka-faced *zomboid*.

"Hydroponix is about to explain how light here in the Solar system behaves," said Sü.

"Green juice?" offered Quizats. He had moved right in close behind them. He could move very quietly when he wanted to.

Zaphine squawked in surprise, and Dork jumped instantly to the 'prancing owl attack' position with a loud "Hai!" Finding no threat, she relaxed, flicking and stretching her arms, and flexing her neck.

"No thank you, Quizats," smiled Alri.

"He's a wily one, that one," said Dork, "it's always the quiet ones, you know. You have to watch the quiet ones."

Nox was impressed. Dork shrugged her shoulders and turned back to look at Hydroponix. Everyone but Nox declined Quizats' offer. Nox didn't like to see Quizats disappointed, and besides, the juice would definitely be top notch stuff. Quizats' eye-lights brightened, as he strutted to a nearby tray to press the juice. He sounded like a paradiddling snare drummer, marching to the best of Scott Joplin and he was singing quietly to himself.

Dork leaned toward Alri. "Is it singing?" she asked softly.

"Yes, I believe he is," whispered Alri.

"Something about a *lovely - lovely - lovely horse*," added Zaphine helpfully.

"What's a horse?" asked Nox.

"A type of bearded robot," whispered Zaphine.

"As I was saying..." said Hydroponix, "the light here is... mysterious."

"Explain mysterious," said Sü.

Hydroponix looked at Sü, "You don't know what mysterious means? That's ridiculous, how did you get to be second in command?!"

Sü raised his eyebrows, narrowed his eyes, and pursed his lips - a look to say, *get on with your story, or I will become seriously vexed.*

Hydroponix smiled and turned back to tap instructions into his BLAC-Adder. They watched as he reproduced a rainbow overhead. Rich, glowing colours intertwined and danced like an aurora, and to make things even more exciting, Hydroponix introduced a piece of music suggested by Quizats. It came through an ultra-high-definition speaker system, which ran throughout the botanical gardens. The sounds from the different musical instruments came from different speakers around the room, and because the hall was damp, and the roof vaulted, the effect was that of a world-class orchestra playing in a galaxy-class venue. It was breath taking. At this moment, the music was the theme from 'Cosmos', by the composer Vangelis. It filled the air, it matched the colourful swirling spectacle perfectly, and it melted Nox's heart. Animals emerged from their hiding places, even Wú gave his habitual sneak attack move a miss and settled gently around Nox's shoulders to listen and watch. Dork was fascinated and kept giving Hydroponix amazed and approving looks.

"The light in this system works in almost the

same way as back on Aleyo, but not quite..." He sucked in his stomach, and puffed up his chest.

Sü looked at Zizsou and rolled his eyes. Unblinking, Garfunkel watched Hydroponix as he spoke, and frowned at him.

"Light travels in waves... BUT... it also travels as particles AND here is the weirdest crazy thing, it changes its behaviour when it is being watched!"

"No! How does light know when it is being watched?" blurted Nox.

"I don't know," said Hydroponix, "but I'm going to enjoy finding out."

Quizats stepped towards the little group. He handed Nox his juice in a silver goblet, and then spoke softly and pointed carefully at the holograms floating above.

"The humans know light does that but they

don't know why. They can't explain it. Humans are a pretty determined lot; I believe they will figure it out sooner or later."

As Quizats spoke, Zizsou jutted his chin out fractionally and folded his arms across his chest. He wasn't impressed. He was concerned. Zizsou did not like a lethal robot on his ship, having opinions on humans or anything else. Robots are tools. They do not have opinions, and they certainly do not believe anything.

Sü knew the captain well enough to know this was serious. Sü was ready for a serious, and possibly even violent call to action. Quizats was making choices, and that made him extraordinarily dangerous. What if he chose to make a hole in the ship for a better view, or if he felt that Alyons are bothersome and should be wiped out! Zizsou began to think of how best to deal with Quizats. Perhaps the time had come to shut him down and send him home.

"I like your leg," whispered Quizats, looking down at Garfunkel's bionic leg, "is that foot real?"

"It is!" said Garfunkel.

"Brilliant," said Quizats with a single firm nod.

Garfunkel smiled at him. Captain Zizsou made his decision. Any person, who would choose to make Garfunkel feel good about himself, is a person worth protecting. He looked at Sü and subtly shook his head, indicating for Sü to hold back. Sü nodded subtly and relaxed.

"That is fascinating Hydroponix," said Zizsou, looking back to the chatty Chief of Science, "what else can you tell us?"

Quizats looked at Zizsou, he quietly took a step back from the group, and turned to listen to Hydroponix.

CHAPTER 14

THAT'S WHY THE IS SKY BLUE

Hydroponix waved his arms, beckoning everyone to gather closely around his desk. He placed a metal rod, a clear beaker, and a jug of water on the desk.

"Yes! Right, good good," he mumbled, his puffed-up chest dropped slightly, and his stomach flubbed out as he stopped worrying about how he looked and became wrapped up in the science. He picked up the rod, waving it as he spoke.

"Every substance has a different refractive index. Light moves through the air. It passes into this container of water and it slows down."

"I don't get it," said Nox.

This time, Sü spoke up. "The refractive index is higher. This means the water is thicker, or solider than air."

Hydro took the rod and gently placed it in to the beaker, poured water into the beaker and suddenly the rod looked bent.

"The high refractive index is what causes the light to bend... and change direction," he whispered, "the rod in this glass looks bent but really it is not." He lifted it out to prove this fact, then put it back into the water.

"And this light, how fast does it move?" asked Alri.

"186,282 miles per *'naughti-Kaylee'*," said Quizats, "more or less." (One naughti-Kaylee being equivalent to one second.)

"So, it takes about - 480 *naughti-Kaylees*, for light to travel the 93 million miles from the sun to the Earth," suggested Dork.

"Yes! There is little to slow the light down,

besides gravitational pull and obscuro - what the humies call dark matter. When light hits the Earth's atmosphere, it slows down whole a lot and the atmosphere scatters the light. Most light goes right on down to brighten the planet surface, but some white light waves and bent blue-violet light waves fill the day sky. So the sky looks pale blue and it glows!" His eyes flashed with delight.

Dork placed one hand on her hip, and swirled the other through the red in the rainbow drifting above her head, "and at sunrise and sunset when the sun is low, we see the less bendy side of the light spectrum through the atmosphere." She flashed another dazzling smile.

"By Gumberguts, you've got it," said Hydroponix, pointing at her.

"Diamonds," announced Quizats. He looked around to check if the others were listening, then went on to explain. "Their refractive index is fantastically high; they slam on the brakes for light like no other known clear substance. Diamond is so dense, that it slows light to half speed!"

Quizats looked around again. He rather liked it when people listened to what he had to say. "They are light traps. That's why they sparkle. That's why we like them. No one shines quite like a diamond. Did you know they are made of carbon; the very thing people are made of? If you put carbon under pressure and turn up the heat, it becomes diamond." Quizats' eye-lights twinkled. "The natural diamonds that exist on Earth today were formed long before dinosaurs, and contrary to popular myth, diamonds are not made from coal. Also, humans can now print diamond. A rather impressive feat I think."

"What about the ring of colours Hydro? You haven't explained the *trixy* ring of colours," said Zaphine. "Why did we see a circle?"

"How come it moved?" asked Nox.

"About that... Dork here was just telling me about a gewgaw she came across on one of her Earth adventures."

"Yes," said Dork, "I've seen a thing that does weird things in sunlight, it may be of some use to you in your studies."

"It could answer some of our questions," Hydroponix glanced at Zizsou, "we need someone to cruise on down to Earth to pick it up. I have pinpointed its location."

Hydroponix looked earnestly at Zizsou, and Zizsou looked back at Hydroponix, and pursed his lips as he considered Hydroponix's new scheme.

"We stop around there all the time for bits and pieces," said Dork, "it's safe enough if you're careful. The people aren't looking for us so they don't spot us. Steer clear of the pets and you'll be just fine".

"Ooh-ooh-ooh," jibbered Nox, with eyes

138

like saucers.

"Eee hmmm," squeaked Zaphine next to him.

Zizsou looked at them, "Alright, take the Paladin."

"Wooo heeheeee!" squealed Zaphine,

"What's the pets?" asked Nox.

"It's a type of hairy cup." said Zaphine, as she and Nox trotted away to get ready for the quest.

Dork's brow furrowed, "are they careful?"

Hydroponix, Zizsou, Sü and Alri looked at one another. Hydroponix 'huffed', slowly swaying his head from side to side as if weighing up his thoughts. Zizsou kept a poker face, Sü laughed, and Alri smiled and shook her head.

"Ah. No. Not really, but they'll learn. Come

on, let's get lunch sorted and after that, you and I can explore your space-ship-shop. I can think of a few *tads and wodges* that would make our engines run like tepid Gallium!" She cackled with unfettered delight; and gabbling like a pair of jolly geese, they strode to the lift.

"What is the pets?" asked Hydroponix.

"Not a type of hairy cup," said Sü.

CHAPTER 15

GET THE GEWGAW

Nox shielded the Paladin Dropship, and Zaphine piloted them high over the Earth's continents.

"The ship is *stealthed*," said Nox, "no-one will see us but Hydro says we're too big to park right near the thing. The place has too many trees."

"Yes. That is why Sü packed sky-bykes," chirped Zaphine.

"He did? Hydroponix said it would be a vigorous stroll from a nearby field. Nearby, meaning far away?"

"Yes. And by stroll he meant run," said Zaphine, " so Sü, being a considerate fella, made a plan. He's a proper chap!"

Nox nodded sagely. "Sü is indeed a groovy

dude." He looked down at the floor-screens of the cockpit to watch the lush countryside flow like a green river beneath them.

"We're there," said Zaphine.

She circled the wood cabin to get a look at the area. It was thick woodland with enormous trees and shrubs. There was a clear space in front of the cabin, but Dork said those areas were no go areas. The humies parked their clunky great vehicles in those spots, and putting a jet there would be wooing trouble. She carefully landed the Paladin about a hundred metres away, in a meadow surrounded by forest, with a path leading back to the house. There were life forms everywhere, flying things and crawling things, woodland creatures great and small, but no people registered on the scanners.

As they unbuckled their safety harnesses, Zaphine wiggled her ears and whispered, "here we go..."

It didn't take long for them to prepare the sky-bykes for action. Zaphine had the BLAC-Adder tablet holstered across her chest, and Nox took charge of the TŌRKA.

"Nox to Copernicus... We are here... The ship is hidden and the sky-bykes are ready to go."

"Confirmed," answered Sü, "we await your next transmission. Stay out of sight."

"We'll be as discreet as a princess's bum burp," said Zaphine sweetly, "Over and out!" She turned and climbed onto her byke.

Nox was revved and ready to go, he connected his goggles to the BLAC-Adder. His goggles showed up the glowing heat signatures of the critters in the bushes and trees, and a turquoise line leading to the target.

"Hydro's co-ordinates are in."

"Let's go!" roared Zaphine.

They took off and raced across the wooded meadow filled with large spring flowers. Because Nox and Zaphine were just about the size of mice, everything was large.

Meanwhile, somewhere between Earth and Mars, a Grumyum spy satellite sent out a signal burst.

In the fetid command room of the Grumyum battle ship hidden behind Neptune, Vague poked at his computer screen.

"I know I saw it. It was something! And it was there."

He twiddled his blue fingers in annoyance at his floating, sky map. The satellite camera zoomed in on an area of forest near Cicely, Alaska. Vague glowed green from the light of the monitor, against which he had jammed his face. He tried to catch another glimpse of *the something*.

"There! I found it. I told you those meddlers would come up on our radar sooner or later, and there they are!" Vague poked the image enthusiastically. It magnified several times. A picture appeared of Nox and Zaphine from above, coasting on the tiny sky-bykes, towards the cabin.

Vague was mystified, "whatever are they after? HAVOK!"

Havok was fiddling with a boondoggle with things on strings and springs, when Vague squawked his name. A bit of the contraption pinged off, hitting him on the forehead, and in surprise and pain, he threw up his arms, legs, and the boondoggle. His chair flipped over backwards and he watched the gadget fly up and come down to hit him hard right between the eyes. He got up and stumbled back to his chair to pick it up. Rubbing his throbbing face, he stooped to pick up the object and whined.

"*Wha'tare* they ever after Vague? I don't

know, I don't undershtand them. They dishcombobulate me. Alwaysh sho bishy-bishy doing what-what who knowsh what. Who caresh?!"

"I dooo," hissed Vague.

On Vague's screen, the two tiny Alyons sped along the path through the trees. The computer calculated their speed and trajectory, and tracked their goal with red markings. Vague zoomed the camera in even closer, to reveal the prize: a magnificent sun-catching crystal dangling from a silver chain in a young maple tree. Target markings blipped around it, and the monitor displayed it clearly.

"There," roared Vague gleefully, "that is what they're after I'm sure of it. Activate the grimdrakes! I WANT IT!"

Vague hit buttons wildly, and Havok caught sight of the crystal on the screen.

"Ooooh, refulgence!" he gurgled and

trotted to his console to help steal it. The Brick emerged from behind Neptune, and with a crackle and pop it jumped the short distance to Earth. At about 400 km from Earth's surface, they released the Grimdrakes. It all happened within a matter of seconds. Three Grimdrakes were ready to go so three Grimdrakes went. They dropped from the Grumyum ship and rocketed into the atmosphere, towards the crystal.

"Attack drakes just hit the atmosphere," growled Sü, "I'm going down!"

"Go!" said Zizsou, "I'll warn the others!"

Nox and Zaphine travelled peacefully unaware as the drakes burned through the air, heading straight for them. They looked up at the fiery trails, wondering what they could be, when Zizsou's voice burst over the TŌRKA.

"Zaphine! Nox! Get back to the ship - GRIMDRAKES!"

"What about the mission?"

"Don't take chances, the drakes are extraordinarily dangerous! Are you nearing the object?"

"Very close, Sir, we can see it. I think we can make it," said Zaphine. She looked at the fire in the sky. "We can do it, Sir."

"It's not wor...." Atmospheric disruption cut Zizsou's voice off.

" Sir?"

"We are cut off, " said Nox, "let's go!"

CHAPTER 16

NO ESCAPE

Zaphine and Nox raced to the crystal. Using a mini laser-blade, Nox quickly sliced the fine silver chain suspending the gewgaw from the tree. He hooked it over his shoulder, and they turned to go. The growl of an engine shook the nearby hedge. It rustled gently, and three fighter drakes blasted through it. Leaves exploded in every direction, and the unmanned drakes charged straight at them. Zaphine and Nox took off like cats from an ice bath, with the drakes chasing after like furious hornets - metal hornets, firing electron bolts. Through the forest, they chased. The sky-bykes were no match for the drakes, manoeuvring up through the high branches, down under half fallen trees and over rocks. The world blurred by. Zaphine's hair whipped her in the face. She ignored it. Losing focus with all these trees around would be disastrous, but they wouldn't last a minute out in the open. They split up, and Zaphine's squeals, shrieks, whooops and eeks could be heard echoing through the forest, as she ducked and dived and loop-the-looped. She whooped with delight when one of the drakes smashed into a tree but glee turned to dread as the tree exploded, and the drake instantly recovered. Nox managed to bring his sky-byke around in a wide curve to get back to Zaphine, just in time. He brought his byke alongside her and a split second later her byke was smashed right out from beneath her, she leapt with all her courage and might onto Nox's byke. With the drakes hot on their heels, the two became more and more anxious. They still had no idea of how to escape these terrible weapons and there was no way to stop them.

Out of the glorious blue Alaskan sky, with blasters blazing, the Phantom swooped in. Just as Zaphine was about to be snatched and crushed by its claws, Sü struck a drake with a sonic disintegrator. Instantly, Sü became the new target. The damaged drake turned to get a shot at this new arrival that was fighting back. There was one highly aggressive grimdrake and it stuck with Nox and Zaphine. It would not allow them gain any distance. It seemed personal. This was because it was personal. This particular drake was controlled by Vague, and with Vague everything was personal. The grabbers were almost touching Zaphine's hair, which swirled out behind her, and it was getting closer. Nox tried to cut the grabbers with the laser-blade but couldn't fight and steer. Zaphine clambered over Nox. She took hold of the handgrips and pulled herself forwards.

"Lean in Nox, stick tight, this is going to get crazy-ace fast."

With her eyes locked on the forest ahead, she reached down and released the panel protecting the inner workings of the jet-byke. While she steered and dodged with one hand, the other hand delicately investigated the connections and wiring inside the byke. She found the impetus couplers and released one, then plugged it into the compression port, and the bike wobbled. Carefully, she locked the protective panel back in place, leaned back and shouted, "LETZA GO!"

Nox's squeals, shrieks, whooops and eeks could be heard echoing through the forest. The byke was now traveling at 120 kilometres per hour, ducking branches, cutting around tree trunks, and nearly taking out a couple of startled wood pigeons. The drake fell behind.

"Whaaat did yooouuuu doooo?" yelled Nox.

She shouted over the screaming engine and roaring wind, "I bypassed the energy regulator, we are burning up the boosters. Can't keep this up much longer, it's going to explode!"

Sü drew two of the three deadly drakes out

into the open above the forest, where he disintegrated the damaged one. The other drake was troublesome. The first drake that Sü destroyed was on autopilot and was predictable, so shooting it was easy. It would take determined focus to destroy Havok's drake. Havok may have been one step beyond madness, but his remote-control skills were nothing short of brilliant! He was unpredictable and quick almost to the point of being psychic about Sü's attacks... but not quite quick enough. One precise plasma blast, combined with Sü's piloting skills, and it was game over for Havok. Sü had a chance to examine the forest below. He could see that just ahead of the last drake, the jet-byke was losing speed. In seconds, the drake grabbers would have them... or they would blow up. He had to act quickly. Forcing the Phantom into a death dive, he aimed directly into the flight path of Vague's drake and fired a vacuum torpedo. He pulled up and the torpedo detonated. The drake swirled into the vortex and with a flash of light, and a shower of tiny metal pieces, bits of drake flittered across the forest like a million silver snowflakes.

Vague roared and threw his controller at the roof in exasperation; it struck the light and bounced right back into his face. Havok stared at the screen and wailed. Vague's tantrum roared on unabated. He didn't know what to do with this rage tearing up his calm, and the more he allowed it to go on, the more it grew. He also managed to break the light and the controller, so now he was sitting in the dark, with no control, and a black eye. This didn't improve his mood at all.

Down on the Earth, and laughing with relief, Sü, Nox and Zaphine came together at the Paladin. After gathering the pieces of Zaphine's byke, and the drake wreckage, they loaded everything into cargo compartments. Nox held the crystal up in the sunlight. Light *spinkles* and mini rainbows danced around them and they quietly watched for a while. Zizsou's voice broke the silence.

"Well done, everyone. Now come home."

"On our way, Captain," said Sü.

The Paladin and Phantom rose above the tall trees, turned and boosted in the direction of the Copernicus. At last, the forest was at peace, the critters emerged and birdsong resumed. Something moved, something that didn't belong. A small, gloved hand picked up a flake of thorium alloy from Vague's shredded drake. The newcomer examined the shard of twisted metal, and pocketed it, then turned on the thick heel of a polished crimson boot and strode back into the forest.

CHAPTER 17

RIDE ON YOUR GOAT BEFORE IT VANISHES!

The Grumyums were defeated and ducked away behind the planet Neptune to rethink and rebuild. Sü had the job of coming up with a plan for how to deal with them. Galactic decrees outlawed any straightforward confrontations even if they were being aggressive. Grumyum lawyers were more lethal than their drakes. Sü had to come up with something good or it could mean war.

That evening, in the main tower of the Copernicus, the Alyons gathered for a situation report, and buffet.

Quizats put on a fabulous spread. The music of Ella Fitzgerald singing, "*It's Only A Paper Moon*", soothed all tension in the Lunar Lounge and lifted everyone's hearts. The crew were all there. Quizats sang softly and swayed gently with the music as he fussed about the buffet table. He knew that sharing the best things with others makes the best things even better and he spared no effort. He wore a baker's hat and a slightly ripped apron. A scrappy beetroot handprint was painted on to the chest of the apron with dribbles of red running down from it, and scrawled across it in cheerful, curly writing, he had scrawled:

BAKER BY DAY

ZOMBIE SLAYER BY NIGHT.

He served assorted teas, fresh-pressed juices with chunks of ice from an ancient blue iceberg, and all kinds of fruit, salads, and sweet and savoury Earth treats that he baked and decorated. Quizats took sugar-glass sculpture to a whole new level. He created a sparkling *feastival* of intricate sugar-crystal birds of paradise, and fantastic beasts, orchids, unicorns, and even warriors fighting edible crystal dragons. The cakes and biscuits tasted as magnificent as they looked, and everyone had at least one in hand and one in mouth. In the centre of the room - the prize. The large crystal gewgaw floated over a sonic hover-stand. A spotlight shone onto it and in every direction, light and colour beamed out. It was like a diamond disco ball, and when touched it would roll and spin slowly above the stand.

"It *is* rather pleasing to the eye," said Alri.

"Hydroponix, will you please explain what all this was about? What is this thing?" asked Zizsou.

Quizats lowered the music volume, so that they could listen properly and focus on the issue at hand.

"Yes-yes-yes. Right. Ok," jabbered Hydroponix excitedly, "we have here the man-made crystal ornament."

Nox purposely placed his face in the path of the rays of colour. He loved the pure colours shining into his eyes, they were completely pure and almost alive.

"What's it made of?" he asked as a very intense blue passed across his face.

"Sand!" exclaimed Hydroponix, "someone super-heated quartz sand, added a little lead oxide, and cooled it slowly. They cut and polished it to shape with many facets, and here you have it - this magnificent thing."

"Which will be returned as soon as you are done with it," said Zizsou.

"Er...yah," agreed Hydroponix, with a smidgen of disappointment, "*anywell*, what we have found is that with a clear object, such as this gewgaw, light is refracted as it first enters the surface of the object. It reflects off the back, and is refracted again as it leaves the object. TWICE

REFRACTED!" He hoped the others would be as amazed as he was. "The light that leaves the object is reflected back over a wide range of angles. This is called DISPERSION."

Images and diagrams hovered in the air around him as he spoke, and pointed.

"Blue-violet is the shortest wavelength!"

"Hydro, what are you saying?" whispered Zaphine.

Sü, had been working on his tablet, looked up.

"He's saying that when white light is sent through something clear, of the right sort of shape, the light waves are split into seven specific colours." He pointed through the colours that ran across Nox's face. "Red-Orange-Yellow-Green-Blue-Indigo and Violet."

"Ride On Your Goat Before It Vanishes!"

blurted Hydroponix, surprising everyone, except Sü, who was waiting for it.

"A Rainbow!" announced Quizats happily.

"We didn't see any crystal when we saw our circle of colours, on our tour through the countryside," frowned Nox.

"No," said Sü, "what you saw was millions of tiny orbs of water; mist in the morning sun and together they had the same effect." He pointed to a close-up picture taken from the exploration flight. "Look. They did what this crystal does. The sunlight goes into each one, - bends a little - hits the back of the drop - and reflects back out. As it leaves, it bends a little more, which causes it to split into the seven colours." Sü pointed to the circle of colour. The position of the sun was exactly behind the ship. "You saw a circle because you were high in the air, between the drops and the sun."

"If you were on the ground, you would have

seen a half circle of colour," added Hydroponix. "You can make one yourself, if you spray a fine mist of water from a hose on a sunny day with the sun behind you.

"Rainbows..." sighed Quizats, "are one of my many favourite things."

Zaphine's eyes sparkled as she watched Nox's face, with the vivid colours moving across it. "Enchanting," she murmured.

Nox's heart skipped a beat.

"There is mention," added Quizats hopefully, "that there are pots o'gold at the ends of rainbows."

"There are no ends of rainbows, old boy," said Hydroponix, patting Quizats on the back with a gentle *clang, clang, clang.* "Rainbows don't exist at a precise place. Their position depends on your position and that of the sun, the rainbow will move whenever you move."

Zaphine was deeply disappointed, "...so we can never touch one."

"Chin up, Zaph," smiled Zizsou, "I have a plan. But first we put the gewgaw back."

"Sir, Dork and Garfunkel are sorting out part of our Grumyum problem," said Alri. "They are out there now, clearing the satellites. Garfunkel is quite belligerent toward Grumyums. He really doesn't like them."

"Beam the *COTS_Demo_Flight* position codes and the like to her so she doesn't target the wrong objects, and please thank her again."

"She's quite a corker," said Hydroponix.

Nox nodded. Zaphine was not interested in what a corker Dork was. Alri smiled and gave her a quick hug, and the crew drifted back to the buffet table for another round of Quizats' *feastival*.

CHAPTER 18

THINGS ARE SELDOM WHAT THEY SEEM

Dork and Garfunkel spent several hours tracking Grumyum satellites. She flew in her golden Halcyon jet, and he in his vanta-black Draak X, following the shadow of night across the planet. It became a jovial plasma blasting competition - who could vaporise the most satellites. Garfunkel won.

Several hours later, the last satellite with jagged Grumyum symbols scrawled across it, drifted silently over India. The Gypsy glided up to it and scanned it. There was nothing of value or interest there so Dork allowed Garfunkel to blast the thing to smithereens. Tiny sparking pieces drifted harmlessly into space, destined to become a spectacular display of shooting stars in the Kalahari Desert night. The TŌRKA buzzed and Zizsou's voice called out from it.

"Pandorka, Garfunkel, you have been a mighty help, thank you. Please do not hesitate to pop in for a holiday if ever you wish it, anything you need, you are always welcome. We have more than enough room."

"No worries love," purred Dork.

"Stay lucky punk," rumbled Garfunkel.

With a brilliant flash of electric violet light, they were away.

Glittering in the gentle late afternoon light, the crystal, hung once again in its spot in the tree. Nox and Hydroponix admired it for a moment, before returning to the dropship. As they took off on their sky-bykes, Hydroponix started to sing; he hurled his head back and forth, making his hair tufts wave like palm trees in an earthquake, all the time stomping his feet on his byke footrests and thumping his hands on the steering-bars. He learned the song from Quizats, and he belted it out at the top of his lungs. It was about a boy called Buddy, who was making a big noise, playing in the street and he was going to be a big man someday, with mud on his face. Apparently, he was a big disc-race (whatever that meant, Nox thought it sounded pretty *hipcool*), Buddy kicked a can all over the place and sang... at this point the song got supremely catchy. Nox was in awe of the thrumming *yheowls* that Hydroponix managed to wrench from his byke engine without blowing it up, and by *gumberguts* it sounded fantastic! By the time they got to the others, Nox *was* completely ROCKED.

Near a small flock of dozy sheep, on a quiet green hill near Cicely, Alaska, the crew of the Copernicus gathered to celebrate their first month in Earth's orbit. Nox and Hydroponix came in on the sky-bykes, and parked next to the little group, who sat on a blanket on the grass, with their backs to the setting sun. They were looking across a green valley with dark clouds gathered on the horizon. Zizsou held up a wafer with blue-red smoke wafting around it.

"Urn'anbert?" he offered hopefully, "Anyone...? ...Anyone...?"

Nox marshalled his courage. "Don't mind if I do," he said nervously.

"Live a little!" laughed Zizsou.

Without breathing in, Nox took a tentative bite. It hit him hard. A tsunami of flavour struck him right in the face. Toffee, hazelnuts, crisp roast potatoes, strawberries and celestial pizza with a dash of glistening melon flooded his sensory universe. It shouldn't have, but somehow it just worked.

"*Ooommmmmnmmm!*" he sighed, through his nose, chewing with large slow bites. He tried not to swallow so that the ambrosia could dance with his heart just a little longer. That was the moment; Nox became a forever-fan of Urn'anbert, the stinkiest cheese in the galaxy.

Zizsou waved the cheese cheerfully at the others.

Hydroponix held up a twirled carrot stick, "I'b fide thaks," he said, wrinkling his nose. He just couldn't do it. His nose outlawed and overruled the very idea! The stuff smelled of a really old cat's breath and goat armpits, or where the pits would be if goats had arms.

Nox leaned over and mumbled to Zizsou, "more for us."

Zizsou winked, and took another bite.

"Ssshhhh," whispered Alri, "the show's about to start."

Quizats chose Anduril - an exquisite piece of music - to play softly from the speakers that he had placed strategically around the area. This had the added benefit of keeping curious sheep at a safe distance, although they formed a wide and woolly circle around the group. They wanted to listen too because, as you now know, animals like music too.

"To enhance the magical atmos," explained Quizats, as he turned the volume up a touch.

Dark clouds loomed in the distance, and as the sun set low, a glorious rainbow appeared. It was so vibrant, and so rich against the dark horizon that Zaphine felt a craving to dive into it and bathe her spirit in the pure colour. They watched in silence, absorbing the music and the snacks and the view.

"Somewhere over the rainbow, by Iz," said Quizats as he fired up a new tune.

It sounded as if the man himself was right there, singing and playing his ukulele just for them. The circle of sheep lay down, and chewed, and listened.

Hydroponix wiped his eyes. "Sweaty," he

explained, nodding at Alri.

Alri smiled at him and wiped her eyes too, then she laughed. It is one of the best laughs, the one you do through, tears with a friend. It really was a very good sound system.

"There are two ways to live your life," whispered Quizats leaning towards Zaphine, "one is as though nothing is a miracle. The other is as though everything is a miracle." He smiled at her, and added, "Albert Einstein said that."

"Did he?" said Zaphine.

"Yes, I believe so," said Quizats, he looked back at the rainbow.

"What about your *pots o'gold?*" asked Zaphine.

Quizats watched the rainbow as he spoke, "I have found that treasure simply depends on my point of view. Moreover, I suggest you hold on to the hope of touching rainbows," he paused, "you just never know."

Zaphine thought about it for a few moments and nodded. Quizats put his arm around her shoulder. She leaned in to the hug and took a bite of turmeric and *poëftaki* curry. She watched the rainbow for a while then looked at Quizats and whispered loudly, "Who's Alf Redeye-Sty?"

That night, Zaphine dreamed of flying over an enormous rainbow, and when she reached the top, she dove in. It felt like a thick fresh mist of dazzling colour - cool, and pure. She held out her hands, and vivid canary yellow poured through her fingers, like water but wasn't wet. She took off, free-flying through a scarlet sky. Sea birds flew alongside, calling softly to each other as an amber sun set beyond a blue, liquid copper, and golden sea, and the rhythmic frosh of the waves gently crashed on platinum sands beneath her.

It felt as real as anything she had felt before or since and became a treasured memory.

Nox also dreamed. He saw six hundred thousand people gathered and singing about asking *Scaramoosh* to do something called the fandango.

Hydroponix dreamed of being on stage, in front of thousands, playing electric guitar, with crystals beaming colours and light on him... and having an alarming amount of curly brown hair cascading off his head, down over his shoulders.

Quizats dreamed of a white unicorn - as usual.

CHAPTER 19

DIG THE MO'

A new day dawned across Europe. Zaphine was out in her Merlin Lightning Bug on a 'gauge and gather' mission, mapping the land, and collecting atomic samples. Her ship was invisible to human technologies and flew in almost complete silence, and because of stealth technology, she was practically impossible for the human eye to see. She could even fly slowly through cities unseen if she so chose but today was a day for the countryside.

In the thrill of the moment, she howled.

"♪ *Gooooood* Morning Planet Earth!"

The wispy morning clouds across the horizon and vapour trails from her jet turned pink and gold as the early morning sun lit the sky. It delighted Zaphine's heart to see it, to hear the bird's morning chorus, and to breathe the cool, clean air. Early mornings are a magical time in the world. Zaphine was scouting the lands of Europe in her Merlin. At this stage, she was under orders to follow a river through the French countryside. As she flew, she sang.

"♫ Let it *gooooo* ♪ let it *gooooooo*..."

"No, Zaphine, *nooooo*! Stop!" wailed Nox, over the voice link.

"*Hey*, be cool there Jumpin'Bean, I'm just diggin' the mo' - Aaaargh! What's this?" she squealed, "eeuw... some sort of giant arachnid trap?"

"What?!" squawked Nox.

It loomed out of the mist ahead of her. Great metal posts towered above her, and cables spread out like web. A huge bridge spanned the river.

"Whoa! Sü, I'm in sector 25-12-1642. There

is a very big construction over this river. I'm going in to check it out."

Sü' watched a screen on his console and waited for Zaphine's Earth images to appear. Captain Zizsou, who was walking around with his cup of red-leaf tea, came over to look at the screen and Nox craned his neck to see. Sü took the completed hologram image and spread it out across the front of the Copernicus Bridge.

"Zaphine is getting excellent metadata here. This is amazing, look at this!"

The suspension bridge appeared as a floating hologram, but patches of it were missing. Quizats walked in with a tray, he paused to look at it too.

It was safe enough for Zaphine to slow down and hover. She flew the Merlin up high, to view the structure from directly above.

"I'm scanning it again. It's huge. Are you receiving this?"

"Affirmative, Zaph. Will you give us a view of it from the east bank please, and do another flyover."

"Sure-*ting* Sü!"

Zaphine did the fly over and the image of the suspension bridge reappeared, this time fully complete.

Sü studied the pictures and measurements, "it might be a good idea to get samples. I'd like to know exactly what it's made of."

"Will do," she chirped, and looked for a good spot to land.

There weren't many cars on the road and

the plants in the area seemed to provide adequate cover, so landing posed no problem. The Merlin turned and landed, and before long, Zaphine was standing on the fine mossy grass, ready for action. She selected a *Helio Plasmic Stasher* from the hold, to pick up and store atomic samples, and activated her goggles. The lenses showed up everything as temperature or life-energy with Alyon symbols in semi circles around the edges of her view. She walked by a frog that was almost the same size as her. It looked at her, and she at it.

The frog said, "Kwaak." It showed up in her goggles as glowing yellow against a cool blue background. The goggles registered thousands of life signs, and so many noises from insects, lizards, and birds all over the place, but nothing big or threatening. Zaphine jogged towards the bridge. Through her goggles, she could see the pressure and tension points outlined. Her goggles lit an area of the bridge that was within her reach and sheltered by trees. She used the *H.P.S.* to drill and gather particles from the parts of the bridge that were highlighted on her BLAC-Adder, and then she made her way back to the Merlin.

"Captain, shall I continue to search for more of these structures?"

"Good idea, Zaph," said Zizsou, "please, do."

"Yes, Sir."

Zaphine activated her engines, and the Merlin took off vertically, then she turned, and turbo boosted her jet across the continent in search of more bridges.

Zizsou sat on the step in front of his desk, chatting with Sü, and drinking tea.

"I've heard some say, - *if you can't beat them join them.* I, on the other hand, am of the opinion that if you can't beat them... dig in your bloody heels and then throw everything and the bathtub at them until you BEAT THEM LIKE BONGOS! Naturally, they will be expecting you to join them so you have the element of surprise! Never give up! Unless they have a nuclear weapon, in which case you need to cobble together a new plan."

"Too true," laughed Sü.

"Captain, I think there is something you should see here on the scanners," said Nox.

He had spotted something unusual in the video footage from Zaphine.

"Yes?"

"Permit me to replay the recording from Zaphine's tri-imager, here," said Nox. He rolled back the recorded footage from the Merlin cameras. The video played until Nox called out and paused it.

"There!" he pointed excitedly. He was

pointing at what looked like a perfectly normal wheat field, on a gently sloping hill.

"What is it, Nox?" asked Zizsou, mystified as to what could have set the little guy off like this.

The image zoomed in, and there it was, the thing Nox had spotted. When he saw it, Sü laughed out loud.

"I remember seeing one of these in our old records, "said Nox. "What does it mean?"

A series of circles had been pressed into a wheat field, with paths at various points connecting them. The shapes were carefully laid out in some unfortunate farmer's field of golden wheat. It looked like the ancient writings of Galifrey, with an elegant, circular design. Such things take patience and great skill to do well and this particular crop circle was magnificent.

"Ha ha ha! I haven't seen one of those since Hydroponix and Q'kadonk drank the fierce sauce!"

laughed Zizsou, "either some humans are playing a trick with some string and a plank, or this field has been visited by old Q on the sauce whilst taking a wee'break from being the scarecrow."

Sü grinned and nodded. He advanced the video to the real-time pictures coming from Zaphine's Merlin.

Nox had lost the plot of what they were talking about and other things were on his mind.

"Speaking of wee'break," he said, "if you'll both excuse me please." He stood up and headed off to the throne room.

Sü and Zizsou continued watching the footage flow in.

CHAPTER 20

ANOMALIES

At his console on the bridge, Sü was following readings and analysing the information Zaphine was sending, and Captain Zizsou was filing reports, when the lights dimmed and flickered. Zizsou looked at Sü and raised his eyebrows.

Sü sighed and shook his head.

"Hydroponix is working on something. He said it's particularly important. He also said, you are not to worry."

Suspicion flash-danced across Zizsou's face. He wasn't sure about the sort of things Hydroponix got up to when one wasn't watching.

Hydroponix was very excited by this new project. He

wore goggles and big gloves for protection as he worked. The large machine he had built in the arbour meadow began shaking, and hissing, and spitting steam. There was a power surge, loud gurgling, and a 'BANG' - quickly, he adjusted the pressure. Cogs and pistons jigged wildly. Hydroponix galloped around to the other side of the machine to watch a small porcelain beaker. For a while, nothing happened. Then dark, steaming liquid oozed from a brass tube. Slowly, it filled the beaker. He used reinforced grip-tongs, to carry the substance to his desk. His tongue stuck out slightly, in focused effort. After gently putting the beaker down, he lifted his goggles to see, and carefully scooped up a thick drop of organic, maple syrup with a micro spoon. He cautiously dripped it into the dark liquid and the syrup vanished.

"Quizats, this is just the sort of stuff that can upset the balance of power across the galaxy!"

"Is it?" said Quizats.

"It is," said Hydroponix.

He slowly poured scalding, frothy, white liquid over the concoction. Sucking a sample into a pipette, he released a drop onto the testing surface of a Handheld Analysis Module.

"Result!" he muttered as he checked the results from the H.A.M, and then gently poured the rest of the liquid into another container, with the words - *"Never Trust An Elementary Particle!! They Make Up Everything!!!"* - scrawled across it. Slowly, Hydroponix removed his gloves. His unblinking eyes remained fastened on the liquid. He gathered up the mug in both hands and sniffed loudly and deeply before taking a teeny-tiny sip. A frothy white moustache settled upon his top lip.

Quizats watched the whole process.

"Is it agreeable?"

After a few seconds, Hydroponix opened his eyes, "Quizats my friend, it's mind-bogglingly agreeable. It's like...like... Madhuri Dixit doing the tango across the strings of my soul."

"Ooohoo. What are you going to call it?"

Hydroponix's eyes searched the sky for a name, as he slowly swirled the magical potion around his mouth. He swallowed. He sighed.

"I shall call it... Quaffee!"

CHAPTER 21

FORCE OF NATURE

Through the course of the day, Zaphine found many bridges. She had been flying around flyovers and aqueducts taking samples from everywhere. She even found a gorgeous little footbridge that was still a living tree, which people had trained to grow across a river.

Meanwhile back on the Copernicus, Nox was visiting the engine room to see how Alri was getting along, and for a chat. He had something on his mind. Talking with Alri was a perk of the job. She was smart and sassy and kind. He liked bouncing ideas, and processing thoughts with her. Confused feelings would somehow explain themselves even if she said nothing at all. It was a weird but groovy skill. She really listened. Not that cheap listening that one gets from people who are just waiting for a gap to fill with their vainglorious opinions. Her listening was the real deal. She left you feeling heard and understood. Moreover, when she spoke, it was gold. He watched her tinkering with one of her machines. *"I want to be able to listen like that,"* he thought. *"It's like a superpower."*

"You have something on your mind," said Alri.

Nox stared at his boot as he herded his thoughts.

"You know with going steady and all that..." He studied his boot laces, how they crisscrossed and zigzagged through the eyelets.

"How can I know if a girl is a true gem or a drama factory? Somebody can be so delightful and wonderful next thing I know, the *bitey* words, and eye rolls come out of nowhere, then she is all nice again and I think it's ok again, but somehow inside feel rubbish. I do my best, and I'm just not good enough and then, I'm embarrassed, and mad and miserable." He watched Alri fuse new parts to a circuit board. "It is so hard to tell if you have a silly gal playing with your heart. You know what I mean?"

Alri watched Nox while she worked on the circuit board, and listened to his story. Then she let him in on what she thought about people.

"I suppose *you* need to figure out what is real, so don't just look at the show. Charm can be *trixy*, and beauty will fade. Find a girl you like, who builds others."

"How do I do that?"

"It's simple. Watch how she treats servers, or cleaners, or beggars... the ones society overlooks - the *'invisibles'* - What is she like when she thinks no one is watching. The truth will out."

Alri tweaked a dial and typed something

188

into her computer then checked the hologram readouts. She wiped her cheek with her wrist, leaving behind a stripe of cog grease.

"Of course, when you find this lovely one in a million, but still imperfect person, treat her with respect and kindness. "

"Yes, I can see how that would work. Ok. So, what if I tell her I like her but she is not interested?"

"You will know what to do."

"Yes. You're saying I must try to win her heart, go around to her house and sing at her window, *make* her like me!"

"No-no, Nox, get on with life, and be a genuine friend. It may hurt but you will be just fine."

"Oh, no, that's hard."

"Find your intellectual match, Nox, find someone who is kind, someone you can laugh with... and *you* be kind. The rest will fall into place."

Quizats stomped in, proudly holding a tray with a mug that had - "World's Best Engineer" - written across it in copper letters engraved with cogs and clockworks.

"Quaffee?"

He offered the mug to Alri. Alri sniffed the air, and dropped her *sprödinger-wranger*.

"I say!" she gasped, "what is that?"

Quizats handed her the mug and watched her face as she took her first sip. With a wink and a nod he whispered to Nox, "apparently, this is the beverage of choice for the modern space Lady."

Nox smiled. He bowed his goodbyes, leaving Alri and Quizats in the Engine room discussing Hydroponix's new brew, and headed back up to the command deck with a spring in his step.

On the command deck, Nox found Captain Zizsou and Sü, looking at a small hologram of a suspension bridge, which hovered in the air between them.

"This is the first structure that Zaphine found," said Sü, turning to Nox, "we're having a look at the construction methods."

Nox circled around the hologram, leaning in close to look at the details of the cables and metal girders holding the roadway in place.

"It looks complicated."

"Humans have come up with ingenious ways to cross rivers and chasms," explained Sü.

"Aces!" said Nox, in a cheeky hipster style.

Sü gave Nox a look to say, *'Cease that sass you grackle!'* Then he went on to explain what Zaphine had found.

"Before deciding on the size and overall look of a bridge, the humie engineers must consider the construction supplies and the distance to be spanned. The challenge is to overcome all the physical forces that threaten to destroy their structure."

"What forces?" asked Nox.

Nox was always interested in everything, and he soaked up information as quickly as an Internet tracker from a quiz for finding out *if you're a Joey, Ross, or Rachel.* (Nox would probably be a Chandler or possibly even a Phoebe.)

Sü tapped the computer. A hologram of a tiny Alyon, in a fluorescent orange onesie, appeared on the desk. The little figure made Nox chuckle. It seemed familiar. Sü, of course, knew it would, because he made it look and move like Nox, when he created it.

The little hologram stood on the desk holding a large weight. It placed the weight on top of a tin can and, as the weight pressed down on the can, the can changed from blue to red, and crushed under the weight. The word "COMPRESSION" appeared, glowing red over the can. They watched the tiny figure tie a green rope onto the weight, and then jog across the desk. It pulled the rope. The rope stretched taught and turned orange, before snapping in the middle. The little hologram man fell over and one of his boots flew off. The word "TENSION" flashed orange over the broken rope. The weight dissolved. An electric-blue outline of a suspension bridge appeared, and the little figure began to blow at the bridge. The bridge twisted in the wind and the twisting parts on the bridge lit up yellow. The word "TORSION" appeared, but the bridge did not fail.

"Great Aunt Nellie!" exclaimed Zizsou, in admiration of the minds and hands that created the bridge, "humans have come a long way."

CHAPTER 22

A BRIDGE TOO FAR

The Grumyums were quiet but not idle. They had been adding cloaking devices to transport shuttles and adapting container pods to look like rocks, traffic cones, and even concrete bollards. Each pod was about the size of a football and there were hundreds of them. Inside each pod, they hid scanning devices, and attack robots, all ready to go on command. For weeks, unbeknownst to the Alyons, the Grumyums shipped the pods to the Earth's surface. They placed them across the planet, in places where they might be useful later. With this phase of their plan complete, they waited for the opportune moment, to strike.

The opportune moment arrived. On the Bridge of the Brick, Vague stared at the console. He was usually in a foul mood, but today he was in a hideous mood. Havok was playing with a piece of snot that wouldn't leave his finger. The more he flicked his hand the more places it found to stick.

"...so Havok," said Vague, "as I said, if there is a rough and nasty crowd, you must join in."

"What if there are two rough, nashty crowdsh, Vague?"

"You join the one with fools that run slower than you, Havok. Use your logic!"

"That'sh why you are the brainsh of the operation, Vague, you're adroit."

"Rude," muttered Vague.

"Be adroit, your planet needs *droits*!"

"Shut up Havok."

The console started beeping. Havok ignored the noise and focused his efforts on getting rid of the snot. It got onto the console, and then somehow made it onto Vague's hand. Vague flung it off, and carried on tapping furiously at his console. The snot was now stuck to Havok's face. He peeled it off, continued swapping the sticky thing between his fingers, and tried again to flick it away. Slowly, he rose from his chair, and moved in behind Vague's chair to get a look at what Vague was doing, he was still absent-mindedly trying to flick the stuff off.

"What is that? What *is* that?" demanded Vague, roughly pressing buttons. He bashed at the console and pointed at a screen, "what is that Havok?"

"I dunno, Vague."

"Hah! It looks like our sky-lens has found something... or... or... someone!"

The Lightning Bug appeared on Vague's screen. It was Zaphine out on her European tour.

"It's the pink and ginger haired one!" growled Vague.

"Let'sh catch it!"

"No Havok we can't be caught with it. Our lawyers are good, but not that good.... Let's kill it."

"...oh. Okay, I concur."

Vague's hidden attack robots waited, and one of them lay right in Zaphine's projected path. Vague's face became a snarling grimace. The screen shone green on him, and his lip curled into a nasty smile. Havok slinked suspiciously quietly back to his seat. At last, the snot glob was off his hands. It was dangling from Vague's earlobe, and wobbling every time he moved, like an enormous, emerald drop earing.

Vague knew this opportunity to strike at the Alyons would soon pass, and he wasted no time. He analysed the movements of the Merlin and worked out the most likely target for her next landing. The Brick hyper-jumped to the far side of the Earth. Vague activated the robot in Zaphine's path, and then sent out his attack drones. Leering out of the front window, Vague cackled with satisfaction, and the snot swung delicately from his ear. Havok looked away, and began to press random buttons on his console, at peace in the knowledge that that snot was no longer his problem.

Italy was glorious. Zaphine had made her way to an ancient Roman stone-arch bridge.

"Sir, I have found another one. It looks quite different to the others, really old, but strong."

"Fascinating. Hydroponix would appreciate more samples Zaph, and I'd like some more angled views of it please."

"Yes Captain, easy-*beez*."

Zaphine circled the little stone bridge, capturing all the angles. She landed the Merlin in a clear area nearby and walked the short distance to the bridge, passed a wild and forgotten vineyard, enclosed by an ancient, stonewall. A little way beyond the vineyard, something lurched, alarmingly quickly, directly toward Zaphine. Between her and the thing, lay the stone wall and wild rambling vines that sprawled across the rocky ground.

She was about twenty feet from the wall, walking back towards the Merlin, with her goggles searching for life signs, and carrying the H.P.S. with its atomic samples stashed safely inside. She stopped whistling. Something felt wrong. The critters of the valley had gone silent. Misty air hung heavy.

Sü' had set a network of warning systems in orbit around Earth, to give time to react to any Grumyum activity and alarms began to go off.

"Zaphine, Grumyums! Get off the ground!" yelled Sü.

Zaphine turned and ran for the Merlin but it was far. The Grimbot reached the wall and without effort, shoved the stones out of its way. It was, coming for her. It leaped at Zaphine but was caught up in vines. Startled and angry, she faced the threat. Through her begoggled view of the world, she saw it storming toward her. Time slowed. Metal feet crunching over stones, charcoal smoke billowing from neck tubes. An armoured robot walker, three times her height, charging at her, getting closer every second. Her goggles flashed warnings. It was now twelve metres away, coming with a singular purpose, to destroy her as quickly as possible. Zaphine bolted. The robot fired an arm cannon. She saw the blast shockwaves and flames licking the air as the missiles left the gun barrel. Zaphine leapt and rolled behind a rock but the rock shattered from the next blast, the pieces of stone tumbled and flew. She had to move or die. She jumped and zigzagged. The robot fired again. The shot hissed passed her ear and hit the tree in front of her. It split and exploded. Splinters slashed in every direction and one pierced her thigh. The spear cut deep and she stumbled and rolled, knocking the rugged splinter deeper. Golden blood flowed and through blurred vision and screaming pain, she stood up and fought on, limping desperately to the Merlin, crying out at every agonizing step. She pulled herself up the ladder and fell into the cockpit. The Merlin lifted off the ground, just as the robot lunged again. Zaphine dodged its grasper claw, but was still within range of the cannons. The robot sprang onto the edge of the bridge and prepared to fire again. Zaphine hovered above for a moment to get a look, dipping to avoid the next missile attack. She fired her laser and with a *crump*, the Grimbot walker exploded.

Sü, who was now fully aware of the unfolding situation, called out.

"Drakes have circled and are closing in on your position from all angles, they will be on you in seconds. If you try to flee, they will destroy you. You must fight!"

Through explosive sobs, Zaphine pulled the blood-soaked splinter from her thigh, and pressed a sterile cloth onto it to slow the bleeding. She tore her trousers away from the wound and sprayed silver antibiotic limpet *gluefoam* on it, then pressed a medic-cloth on to hold it closed. Finally, she secured it tightly with boss tape. To quiet her shaking, she wolfed down a maple biscuit and tea from a flask and the shock subsided. Zaphine turned to face the drakes and used the pain to focus her mind - it was time for a fight.

"There are five of them," announced Zizsou, "here they come."

Zaphine rocketed into the sky.

"Focus, Zaph," said Sü calmly, "you have got this. One at a time: take them out."

CHAPTER 23

THE GRASSY KNOLL

It was Zaphine's Lightning Bug against five Grimdrakes. She would have to be fast. Chance of death grew every second she was in the air with even one of these things. They moved in formation and kicked off their attack. The Merlin weaved like a swallow, and turned on a wingtip, avoiding the strikes from the electro pulse cannons. An electric storm swirled around her, lightning bolts from the cannons scorched everything in their path. She spin-dived, looped the loop and spiralled. The Grimdrake fighters were no match for Zaphine's superior flying skills, but they weren't clumsy either and they only needed to hit her once. Zaphine's nifty manoeuvring nearly caused two of the drakes to collide; they adjusted quickly and locked on to her heat signature. One of the drakes was about to launch a firestorm missile, when a plasma beam discharged from a shrubbery on the grassy knoll below, and obliterated the two drakes with one shot. One of the remaining three drakes fired a flurry of missiles but instead of hitting the Merlin, the missiles struck another drake. Zaphine flew through the ball of blue fire, blasted another, and corkscrewed straight at the last fighter. Just as it powered up to fire at her, the Merlin's wings sliced it, and the drake spiralled to the Earth in two neat pieces. Within 27 seconds, the battle was over.

Nox was standing, his fingers white as he gripped his desk, and through hot tears he watched the incoming footage from the Merlin. He didn't realise that he was shouting.

"Excellent, Zaphine, sweet shot!" he wailed.

"Most impressive," said Sü.

"Come home Zaph, we don't know what

else they have out there," said Zizsou.

"Sir, I didn't hit all those drakes. There was... I... I don't know what happened!"

"Sü will be down later in the Paladin to clean up," said Zizsou, "he will figure it out."

"Ok," replied Zaphine, and she set course for the Copernicus.

In the mayhem of the moment, no-one had actually seen the plasma beam firing from the grassy knoll and because of the battle interference or some sort of shielding, Sü's sensors didn't pick it up either.

In the medical bay, Alri cleaned and patched Zaphine's wound and Nox stood close by to give support. Zaphine was worried.

"There was something weird going on down there, Alri. I didn't shoot all of those drakes."

"Yes, I know," said Alri. "I looked over the battle record and there was a moment when the sensors jammed."

"What? How? *Who?!* Was it Grumyums?"

"No, Nox, whoever it was, was against them."

"That's good! The enemy of my enemy is my friend," said Zaphine.

"Not necessarily," said Alri, she blinked slowly and smiled, "the enemy of your enemy could be a whole lot worse than your enemy."

Hydroponix and Quizats stood by the open-air lab desk.

"Quizats, stop fussing, and connect the cable so we can send the information Captain Zizsou asked for."

"Undignified is what this is," muttered Quizats and connected himself to the console. Holograms of incredible human creations, floated around the room. The Great Pyramid of Giza, and the Great Wall of China hovered by his head.

"Do we have to do this?" he huffed, as the Taj Mahal swished by.

"It would be helpful," said Hydroponix soothingly, tapping the pyramid to reveal a detailed inside view of it, including the secret chambers, filled with dazzling treasures.

"What if I don't feel like it?" said Quizats.

"Alri would like it," said Hydroponix casually, as he carefully examined the Eiffel tower. It even had tiny little hologram people on it, looking out at him through tiny telescopes and pointing.

Quizats paused for a long time to process this - about 0.0023 seconds - which is a very long time for this robot to think about anything. A happy Alri was one of the things that made Quizats happy.

"Ok," he rumbled, and reached out to the hologram of the London Eye to give it a cheeky spin. The little hologram people inside the pods held on to tiny railings and stuck to the sides of the pods as they spun.

Later that day, everyone gathered on the Copernicus Bridge for a briefing about the new discoveries.

"Hydroponix," said Zizsou, "show us what you have."

"And me," added Quizats firmly.

Zizsou corrected his request. "My apologies. Quizats and Hydroponix, show us what you have. Please."

"I have cross-referenced the pictures from

Zaphine's mission with the information Quizats collected from the wonder wonderweb, and I came…"

"*We*," interrupted Quizats, and nodded sagely.

"*We* came up with this," said Hydroponix.

The floating images of the mightiest and most spectacular human constructions ever built drifted amongst the crew. Suspension, cantilevered, beam and truss bridges appeared. Hydroponix explained how each worked; their strengths, weaknesses, and what they were made of.

"The newer buildings are made of concrete, glass and steel," explained Hydroponix holding out his hand to pat the hologram of the Sunrise Kempinski Hotel.

"People have created all sorts of wonderful things - quite resourceful really."

Nox turned to Zaphine. "I don't want buns of steel..." he declared, "I want buns of cinnamon!" He smiled awkwardly and Zaphine looked puzzled. Nox quietly turned back to Hydroponix, and tried to look fascinated.

"What is concrete?" asked Zizsou.

"Concrete is a man-made stone," replied Sü, "it is made by mixing lime, clay, sand, gravel and water."

"What is lime?" asked Alri.

Before anyone else had a chance, Quizats answered, "lime is what you get when you burn limestone or marble. Evidently, people have been using concrete for over 7000 years. Very strong stuff, especially when it is reinforced with steel rods. That is how they build those towering structures in their cities.

"Ah, right. Thank you," said Alri.

"I have a reasonably decent idea for a jolly," announced Captain Zizsou.

"What are buns?" asked Zaphine.

Later, when there came a quiet moment, Sü called Captain Zizsou aside.

"Captain, I went down to collect the drake pieces. One of the drakes is gone."

"That is alarming! You're certain it wasn't vapourised in battle?"

"Yes Sir, those were accounted for. The sliced drake disappeared," said Sü, "and two of the drakes were not shot down by Zaphine... nor by another drake."

"How do you know?" asked Zizsou.

"I found plasma burns on the pieces.

The attack robot parts are gone too."

"Go over the accounts, Sü, and find out exactly what happened. I don't like mysteries."

"Yes, Sir. I'm on it, and I have contacted Dork. She and Garfunkel are already going after the sleeper Grimbots that were hidden across the planet."

"They seem to enjoy upsetting Grumyums as a hobby," said Zizsou, "I wonder who has the most hits."

"I believe Garfunkel is winning, Sir."

CHAPTER 24

IT'S A WONDERFUL LIFE

On a cloudless spring afternoon in the Hunan Provence of China, the seven tiny citizens of the Copernicus perched on a spectacular glass bridge. As high as the Eiffel Tower, it crossed over the Zhangjiajie Grand Canyon, and swayed slowly in the mellow breeze. There were no people around on this day; the bridge was theirs alone. Through the green valley far beneath danced a river. It was so far below that it looked like a silver glitter pen line snaking through biscuit crumbles. Captain Zizsou looked over the landscape and breathed the soft warm air deeply; it carried the scent of orange blossoms. He listened to the call of the birds, and the babble of his happy crew as they chatted about life, the universe, and everything. They ate snacks, and sipped tea in lively fellowship. Everyone called it tea now rather than cha, because Quizats insisted. He felt that no other word puts a smile on the face, or boosts the spirit the way the word tea does. The word 'Aces' comes close; it has the *zazz* but not the *zing!*

Nox sat straight-backed, with his legs crossed beneath him, and nibbled a freshly baked cinnamon bun while he listened to Zaphine share her adventures. He watched her wave her mango sorbet lolly, and recall the dangers and wonders she encountered. Her wound was healing well but she still walked with a limp, and it freaked him out that they came so close to losing her. This is not what they signed up for, there was no talk of Grumyums when they signed up... and yet, he admitted to himself, even if they knew all, nothing in the verse would have stopped them joining this mission.

Alri and Hydroponix were in deep discussion about the significance of the number 42. Even Quizats was taking pleasure in the moment, soaking up the scene, the sounds, and the sun.

Zizsou's mind was unsettled and elsewhere. Those Grumyums really were a serious threat. Where did the missing drake and robot go? Even more concerning was - who fired the shot from the grassy knoll? Whoever it was could just as easily have destroyed the Merlin or any one of the jets. Zizsou was pleased that Sü managed to figure out what had happened. What vexed him was that there were worse things out there than Grumyums.

"We must dig to the bottom of this Sü."

"We will, Sir."

Captain Zizsou nodded, satisfied in the knowledge that Sü was on the job. He took a large bite of crunchy wafer and Urn'anbert - the stinkiest cheese in the Galaxy.

Quizats stood up and strutted over to join Zizsou, together they looked across the valley, and at the sky.

"This really is a beautiful day," said Quizats, "even with that dark cloud lurking way over there. Ah well, it's a good thing that it's small and far away."

Zizsou nodded and put his hands on his hips and frowned at the little dark cloud.

"The thing about the most powerful things, Quizats, is that they always start small... and they move faster than you'd expect."

"Yes. That is true." Quizats' gaze wandered down to the great river dancing over the rocks so far below, his eye-lights brightened and he bellowed, "Who's for a game of Poo sticks?"

MORE STUFF ...

Alyon - Alphabet

"...stop freaking yourself out."

The waters of the English Chanel were calm...

"We've got to get out of here!"

"Eeuw, it's some sort of giant arachnid trap!"

"Zaphine, Grumyums! Get off the ground!"

REFRACTION

Light is like a vehicle that hits
   gravel   - the wheel
that hits it first will slow,
causing the vehicle to
turn toward that direction.
In the same way, if light hits
a substance with a higher
refractive index, to one side
it will bend to that side.

*Light travels in waves and
as particles, and behaves
 differently when it is
being watched!

When light refracts in a prism, it splits into colours of the rainbow because some wavelengths bend more than others.

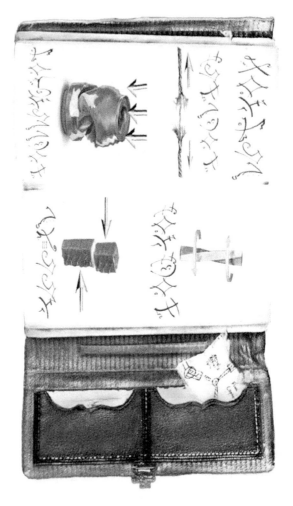

Hydro's notes on forces.

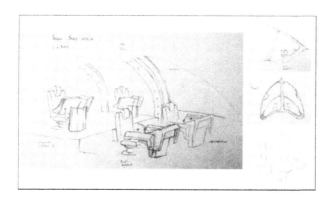

229

THE NINE PILLARS OF LORE

BUILD UP WITH YOUR WORDS
AND SPEAK YOUR TRUTHS RESPECTFULLY

DO NOT TAKE NOR MAKE LONGING EYES
AT WHAT BELONGS TO ANOTHER

DO NOT DELIGHT IN DESTRUCTION

PONDER ON WHAT IS GOOD
AND CHOOSE GLADSOMENESS

RESPECT AND PROTECT
ALL WORLDS YOU ENCOUNTER

DO NOT CAUSE SUFFERING

PROTECT THE WEAK

NEVER WASTE LIFE

BE KIND

For more wild adventures
with the indomitable
ALYONS

Printed in Great Britain
by Amazon